ENDGAME

And the seconds were ticking away, drawing them inexorably closer to disaster. Four days, that was all. Four short days till the deadline expired.

The tune on his Minidisc had just cut down to a drum-only breakbeat when the tears came.

It only made things worse. Every time he had cried in the past – and he was not a cryer by nature; it took a lot to bring him to that point – he had always felt better afterwards. Something about the release of tears seemed to let off the pressure, made it all not so bad. This time, long after his tears had been wiped away on a corner of his blanket, the suffocating sensation remained. The tightness in his chest, his throat, the pounding in his head.

There
was
no
escape.

Point

ENDGAME
Chris Wooding

■ SCHOLASTIC

Scholastic Children's Books,
Commonwealth House, 1-19 New Oxford Street,
London WC1A 1NU, UK

a division of Scholastic Ltd
London ~ New York ~ Toronto ~ Sydney ~ Auckland
Mexico City ~ New Delhi ~ Hong Kong

First published in the UK by Scholastic Ltd, 2000
This edition published by Scholastic Ltd, 2003

Copyright © Chris Wooding, 2000

ISBN 0 439 97888 2

Printed by Nørhaven Paperback A/S, Denmark

10 9 8 7 6 5 4 3 2 1

"For us to use the weapon would therefore be equivalent to more than suicide: it would be genocide – the extinction of our race – in the literal and precise meaning of that much abused expression."

Enoch Powell

" The song is almost over now and we've nothing left,
  To place upon these fires, they are dead,
  And I've still got this place in my hands,
  How are we, how are we ever gonna solve this mess?"

Vanilla Pod: 52 Card Pick-Up

"That was a special news bulletin from Brussels, brought to you by our correspondent, Andrew Gough. Now the weather with Sean Leary."

"Thanks, Jane. Well, sun-lovers will be pleased to know that our unseasonably early start to the summer shows no signs of breaking up. After a scorching June, the coming month looks set to be even better. In fact, local authorities are considering a hosepipe ban to preserve the reservoirs in the face of what looks like being a very long hot spell. A little rain up in Scotland, and a few wisps of cloud from this straggly band in the southwest here, just grazing Cornwall on its way to Europe; but overall, today will be sun and more sun, with top temperatures all the way up to thirty-three around Brighton. The temperatures will stay up during the night, but humidity is low, so it should keep on the right side of muggy until tomorrow morning. Tomorrow *much like today, the band of cloud gone completely from Cornwall, and we're looking at yet another hot Friday, if only fractionally cooler than today, with highs around thirty-one, thirty-two. Burn times will be short, fifteen to twenty minutes in some areas, and for hayfever sufferers, I'm afraid it's going to be a bad few days for you. Early next week things will become more unsettled, possibly with some rain coming in there; just a little British stutter before the real heat hits. But for the first part of the weekend . . . keep that sun cream ready."*

"Thank you, Sean. We'll be back at four. From all the team, see you then and have a good day."

It was a rare cloudless day over Sheffield, at the height of the hottest July in history for what seemed like the third or fourth year running, and the tarmac baked in the rays of a fierce sun. Even the cars seemed sluggish, scorching bonnets flashing dazzling light as they meandered through the arteries of the city. Children licked at ice-creams, the cones gone soft and slick with runnels of melt and their fingers saccharin-sticky with raspberry sauce. Long-haired dogs sweltered in the shade with their tongues lolling, envying their shorter-haired cousins who scampered around the parks, excited by the profusion of people who had come out to enjoy the sun.

For a day that was to be one of the most dread-laden in living memory, it could scarcely have been less appropriate. Nature has no respect for history.

Wren sat at his desk and gazed out of the classroom window over the city. Sacred Heart R C stood halfway up the broad flank of one of the great hills that Sheffield was built on, and from where he sat he could see the streets and buildings plunging into a valley and clambering up the other side, half obscured by the dense green foliage of the trees. Over there was Nether Edge, almost invisible beneath its canopy. Hunter's Bar nestled somewhere distant, follow Ecclesall Road to the town centre. . . He plotted a route out in his head, a map of his escape from the utter pointlessness of fourth-period maths. Thirty-five minutes, half as long as most of their lessons, because the local council had decided that now there had to be nine periods a week instead of eight for an A-level course. It usually took them fifteen to settle down, and the rest of the time was spent waiting for lunch break. Even the teacher recognized that he was waging a losing battle and let them out early every week. Why was every form of government or authority made up almost exclusively of retards?

It was too hot to work, anyway. Too hot even to bother whispering to each other, when they were supposed to be doing an exercise on algebraic fractions while the teacher marked submissions he should have done a week ago. The sound of sighing, the mutter of a doodling pen and the occasional shriek of a chair leg across the varnished wood floor formed the backdrop to Wren's daydreaming, and he had nearly fallen asleep by the time the uninterested teacher told them they could go for lunch.

Jamie was waiting by the classroom door when he came out. He'd had a study period – which to anyone in the sixth form meant sitting in the common room for an hour and reading discarded copies of Minx and J17 – and had decided to cut it short to meet Wren before his girlfriend Kayleigh found him and dragged him off somewhere.

"Alright, Wren," he said, collaring his friend as he walked past.

"What's up?" Wren replied rhetorically.

"Another productive maths lesson?" Jamie asked, as they joined the flow of students cascading down the stairs towards the schoolyard.

"Once more I leave the room enlightened as to the total lack of bearing that advanced mathematics has on real life," Wren replied.

"Two more weeks, if that," Jamie said. "And it's gonna be a fine, fine summer. You can take it."

Wren made a face that said: *not a lot of choice in the matter, have I?* and they pushed through the double-doors and out into the sun.

They were no more unusual a pair than most that could be found in any Sheffield school. Wren was not short, but his stocky build made him seem smaller than his five feet eight, and standing next to Jamie – who was clear over six feet by a good few inches – was an unfavourable contrast. Jamie wore rectangular glasses and had short-shaved, mousy brown hair; Wren's blond was buried, as always, under a baseball cap worn backwards. Wren wore baggy and loose skate-clothes and a necklace of wooden beads that clung tight to his thick neck like a choker; Jamie wore more pedestrian attire, earth tones and unremarkable shoes. Both of them had rucksacks growing out of their backs.

"You going down the vil?" Jamie asked, confident that he'd get a yes in reply. "The vil" was the catch-all term for anywhere off school grounds. It had probably been shortened from "village" somewhere back in the hazy fug of history, but why it applied in the centre of a city was anyone's guess. Student slang, like teachers, rarely followed the laws of logic.

Wren mumbled an affirmative. After nearly six years of seeing the same playground, and watching the new crops of Year-Seven kids get ever more cocky and irritating, he would take nearly any other option rather than stay at school for lunch break.

"Mayner said he'd meet us there," Jamie supplied.

"Okay, whatever," Wren said.

"You alright?" asked the other, as they trudged across the yard towards the school gate. There were only a few pupils out at the moment, and most of them were heading the same way; the bell had not yet rung for lunch.

"Yeah, I'm just a little spaced," Wren replied. "Classroom was like an oven. I was halfway to dropping off."

"You not sleep last night?"

"Not much. I was worried about . . . y'know."

"Kayleigh's dad? You *still* on that?"

"I dunno," Wren said, scratching the back of his neck beneath the bill of his cap. "Not usually. Just last night, I couldn't sleep for thinking about it." He caught Jamie's slightly sceptical look and frowned. "She's my *girl*friend, Jamie. I'm *supposed* to be concerned about her dad."

Jamie drew a can of Pepsi from the side-pocket of his rucksack and popped it. "You've only met him once in the whole time you've been seeing her," he pointed out. "How long is it now, anyway? Two years?"

"Just over *one* year," Wren said over the ascending slurp of Jamie's attempt at drinking. "And he's in the army, so of course I never meet him. He's never around."

"You know this whole military build-up thing is just gonna wash away," Jamie assured him with casual confidence. "Nobody'd dare have a war nowadays. Not like a proper one. Soon as anyone started losing, they'd just nuke the shit out of whoever was beating them. Then there'd be the retaliation and *bam*!" – he shrugged – "no more human race."

Wren couldn't be bothered to debate the point or explain the source of his strange fear. In fact, to be honest, he didn't know himself. Kayleigh's dad was stationed in a trouble hotspot, that was true enough; but there was no more reason to worry now than there had been three weeks ago when it all began. Sure, things were looking bad in the Far East. Russian Federation Forces were massing to the north of the Philippines, and NATO forces had been deployed there as a deterrent, Kayleigh's dad included. But he was smart enough to know that the media had a tendency to blow things out of all proportion, and so he took any major world crisis with a healthy dose of salt.

It was all he could do. The alternative was too dire to contemplate.

They met Mayner outside Turner's Deli, which was

nothing more than a sandwich shop with a misleading name. It sat in a small, paved square, surrounded by off-licences and sweet stores and an amusement arcade. The combination of food, drink and games made the little plaza a powerful lure for those Sacred Heart pupils who were old enough to be let off the grounds or canny enough to sneak out. There were already a good few there by the time Jamie and Wren arrived, mainly Year Tens who had skived their fourth period.

Mayner looked like one of the youngest there, even though he had a good two years on most of the kids that hung around in clots, smoking or stocking up on E-numbers to make it through the afternoon. He was cursed with babyish features and clear skin, and was still unable to grow facial hair. In twenty years' time he would probably appreciate it, but right at the moment he hated the face and body that his parents had given him. He was also small and scrawny, which only conspired to make him look even younger. The amount of times he had been asked for ID at the cinema or when buying a pack of tabs was truly humiliating. And his size made him a natural target for mockery and other, more physical attention.

"Kayleigh not with you?" he asked as they arrived.

"Can you see her?" Jamie replied.

Mayner didn't deign to answer, just fired up a Marlboro Light and looked past him at something on the other side of the plaza.

"Son of a *bitch*, I'm bored," he said at length.

"You'd be less bored if you ever bothered turning up to lessons," Wren commented.

Mayner gave him a look. "Pause, reflect, and think about what you just said."

Wren did so. "You're right. I take it back."

"Can't all be overeducated cynics like yourself, y'know," Mayner added.

"What does *that* mean?" asked Wren. "Overeducated? You mean 'cause I read during the day instead of watching soul-withering American import chat shows about people getting in touch with their inner child by talking psychobabble that even *they* don't understand?"

"That's the Wren we know and love," said Jamie, slapping him on the back. "Why say something simple when you can be complicated and long-winded?"

"You guys are sweet, you really are," Wren replied, smiling at their observation. He shaded his eyes and looked up at the glaring sun above them. "I'm gonna get a drink. Back in a minute." He slid inside the off-licence.

"Too hot for school," Mayner said, dragging on his cigarette. He ran a hand through his floppy, centre-parted brown hair and squinted at Jamie. "Can't be arsed."

"Yeah," Jamie replied neutrally, thinking that he could do with something from the shop himself but unable to decide what he wanted. The Pepsi he'd just drunk had made him thirsty.

They spent their lunch hour talking about things of little consequence to any of them, recycling slanderous gossip from their classmates in the full knowledge that none of it was true. School had lost its edge. Back in the pre-GCSE days, when everyone had been a torrid mess of awakening hormones and nobody was experienced enough at schoolyard politics to keep their secrets to themselves, lunch hour had been a hotbed of rumour and subterfuge. Couples were made and broken, lies and staggering truths were exchanged, revelations were discovered or manufactured. Now what was there? It seemed that life had ground to a halt while they slogged through their A-levels, and nothing new or exciting was going on any more. The focus of school life had moved away from the playground and into the bars and nightclubs and parties of Sheffield, and Sacred Heart had been demoted from a social gathering-place to a dry prison where the only alternative to boredom was education.

Despite all this, the unusual announcement in the common room at the start of fifth period did little to excite them. A special assembly would be held in the hall for the last period of the day, by the order of the Head. Attendance was mandatory.

This, at least, gave the pupils something to speculate about for the next hour and forty-five minutes. The Year Sevens could think of nothing else, offering wild theories as to what might have prompted such an unprecedented event. The upper years didn't care. There had never been an assembly in the history of Sacred Heart that had been anything less than a waste of time.

Last period came, and they filed into the assembly hall. A teacher at the door shushed them as they walked in, which stopped their mutterings for at least ten seconds before they started up again inside. The sixth form was at the back, a swipe of colour against the dull grey-and-crimson uniform of Sacred Heart. Wren and Jamie stood next to Mayner, who had decided to come to school for the afternoon. The atmosphere ranged from naked excitement at the front of the hall to studied disinterest at the back as the tall, besuited form of Mr Renford walked slowly across the stage to the microphone.

Their head teacher commanded a remarkable amount of respect from the pupils, considering his position. He was in his early sixties, and physically he was the perfect picture of a crotchety old man, with his thin body, sunken cheeks and wispy white hair that had receded from his scalp. However, he was also scrupulously fairminded, and remarkably good about listening to pupils' opinions and acting on them. He had gained a reputation for being "just about alright", and so craftily deflected the hatred of the student body on to his deputy head, Mrs Kidd, who deserved it.

"Good afternoon," he said, his voice coming from six separate speakers around the hall, followed by a short, tinny echo. The pupils rustled into silence.

Mr Renford surveyed the room with his heavily-lined eyes. "Most of you, I'm sure, are wondering exactly why I have called this special assembly," he said, his words slow but certain. "Many of you will undoubtedly be happy at the chance to finish early. You will be pleased to know that I intend to make this short, and you may then have the rest of the period to yourselves."

The first years muttered excitedly. Little touches like this kept Renford on top.

"To be honest," he continued, with something like a sigh, "what I have to say now you will all know by tomorrow, or even by tonight. I intend to give you the facts to prevent any wild rumours and speculation. You have all heard, I suspect, about the build-up of Russian Federation forces and their allies in the Pacific."

Wren felt a shiver run through him, as if the sun had suddenly darkened for a moment.

"At around midday today, the announcement was made that an invasion has begun. Troops from the Russian Federation, Mongolia, China and Kazakhstan have stormed beaches all across the Philippines and Malaysia. NATO forces that had been posted there for defence have been overrun."

Wren looked around for Kayleigh, suddenly alarmed, but he couldn't see her. He felt suddenly guilty about having neglected her that day.

"Those of you that have been following the news more closely will know that NATO had threatened to intervene if the suspected invasion should occur. As of two o'clock this afternoon, they issued an ultimatum to the Eastern Alliance, giving them exactly one week to withdraw their troops and demobilize before NATO enter the zone of conflict to expel them. I'm sure you can imagine what this might mean."

Jamie felt his chest tighten a little. He glanced at Mayner, who seemed blandly unconcerned. It sparked a momentary pang of annoyance. Mayner had never cared about the greater concerns of the world; he had this incredible ability to think no further than the immediate future, and then only about himself. But this wasn't just another stock market crash or oil spill. They were talking about *war*.

"Those are the facts as we know them," Renford was saying, craning forward over his microphone. "I would urge you all to take a special interest in news broadcasts from now on. Civil defence bulletins may be issued. It would be in your best interests to listen to them. Please bear in mind that there is a very great possibility that this whole affair will come to nothing, and I would advise against paying attention to alarmist tabloid headlines. The BBC World Service and the television news is your best source of information. Additionally, this does *not* mean school will be cancelled tomorrow, or next week. We will be especially hard on truants."

Nobody even had the heart to utter the obligatory groan at the news. Most of the pupils took the announcement well enough, being unaware of the full implications of what was happening; but the suddenly grave ambience in the hall had made them quiet and serious.

"My daughter has a saying," Renford said, after a moment. "She says: 'Trust in God but lock your car'. We have faith that our Lord will see to it that no harm comes to us, but we must do everything we can to cooperate with the authorities in this time of crisis, and we must see to our own safety and that of our families. For now, let us pray with the words that Jesus taught us. Our Father. . ."

The pupils joined in on the second phrase, unconsciously pausing between words and adding emphasis in perfect time with each other, trained by repetition. The hall resounded with the low swell of the prayer, punctuated by the sharp hiss of the susurrants. Nobody was even hearing the words as they said them. Every mind in the hall was awhirl with other thoughts. Those that did not appreciate the importance of what the head had told them were uneasy at the warnings he had given, and were beginning to suspect that something really serious was afoot. Others, especially those who took History as an A-level, were recalling words and phrases that they had thought were consigned to the past, and ones they thought they would never really have to consider. In the space of a few sentences, it had suddenly become frighteningly possible.

The Blitz of London. The Cuban Missile Crisis. Hiroshima and Nagasaki.

World War Three.

CHAPTER TWO

"Now with the story behind the headlines, we have Andrew Gough, our correspondent in Brussels, where the NATO summit is being held. Andrew, what's the real reason behind the invasion of the Philippines and the surrounding islands?"

"Well, Jane, that's precisely the question that has been asked all over Brussels for the last three weeks, ever since the military build-up began. All I can say is that there are no clear answers as yet. If any reason has been ascertained by NATO, then they are certainly keeping very quiet about it. It has been speculated that the leaders of that organization are as much in the dark as we are. Certainly, our best analysts have been unable to come up with an adequate reason as to why four countries that, in combined size, are comparable to the entire continent of Africa, should take such an interest in a string of tiny islands on the equator."

"And their interests appear to be greater even than that, isn't that right?"

"That's exactly right. Countries such as Vietnam and Cambodia are demanding military assistance to counter the ground forces that are moving in their direction from mainland China. Troops are on the alert in northern Australia, and it has already been presumed that Indonesia and Papua New Guinea will be next on the list for the Eastern Alliance. Fleets from the Russian Federation have been sighted crossing the Indian Ocean towards Somalia and Kenya."

"And have NATO made any comment on this?"

"NATO have made a comment on what one diplomat called 'an unacceptable and aggressive acquisition of territory'. They had resolved several days ago that they would take a firm stance against the Eastern Alliance if their military posturing should turn into an invasion, and this is why their response to the attack on the Philippines has been so swift. The one-week deadline was agreed then, and as of two o'clock Greenwich Mean Time, it has been put into effect. If the Eastern Alliance do not pull out their troops and return to their military bases, NATO will intervene with – and I quote – 'all necessary and prudent force'."

"Speculation is still rife as to why NATO have chosen to involve themselves in this matter at all, when the conflict in the East does not involve any of their member countries. Have there been any further developments there?"

"NATO has been restructuring itself ever since the Cold War ended in order to adapt to peacekeeping and crisis *management in cooperation with non-member governments. They maintain that they are intervening in response to a cry for help from the endangered countries."*

"But is that the whole truth?"

"Many critics think not. For an alliance like NATO to square up against the might of the East, there would have to be a much more pressing and urgent reason than the one they have given. What that reason is remains to be seen."

"Finally, Andrew – with two great alliances set to go head-to-head with each other, are we looking at the possibility of a World War?"

"It's really too early to say, but analysts have been reported as saying that this affair is more dangerous even than the Cuban Missile Crisis of 1962."

"Which is, of course, when the United States – led by President Kennedy – and Khruschev's Russia came to the brink of war over nuclear missile bases in Cuba."

"Only a last-minute back down by Russia saved the world from conflict then. We can only hope that the same will happen here. But one thing is for sure: if any backing down is to be done, it won't be by NATO."

"Andrew Gough, thank you very much."

"Thank you."

"I mean, World War Three? What're you on? It even *sounds* dumb. Like a sequel to a crap action flick."

"Damn, lucky we've got your spot-on social observations to keep us safe, Mayner," said Wren, not taking his eyes off Kayleigh, who was walking with them. "I was getting worried there."

"S'no problem," Mayner grinned. "Happy to help."

Wren's mind was not on Mayner, and he wasn't really listening to his chatter as they walked their route home from school. It was still a beautiful day, and the streets and alleyways swam with heat. The cars glided by on their left as they walked along the wide pavements, flanked by high walls of weathered stone and shaded by overhanging branches. Their path took them through some of the nicer districts, and on a day like this it would have been pleasant, if not for the announcement made half an hour earlier in the school hall.

Wren studied the girl at his side. She was tall, about an inch taller than him, with long, wavy blonde hair that fell unhindered on either side of her face to mid-back. She dressed like a grunge kid, a look that had been years out of fashion: a floral dress worn over a vest, combined with striped black-and-white tights and red Doc Marten's. It was her insistence that the fashion had been dead long enough to be classed as retro, so she had taken it as her own. She was an individual, to say the least, which was what Wren liked about her.

Her face was a little long, the bones a little too pronounced to be called conventionally pretty; but Wren was of the opinion that most conventionally pretty girls were as interesting as rock salt, so that was fine with him. He loved the way she tossed her hair when she laughed; the way her fingers interlocked perfectly with his when they held hands; how her lips were never dry when they kissed, unlike his – he stole the moisture from her.

But she was silent now, the signs of worry plain on her face, watching the pavement and only meeting his eyes for as long as necessary. He didn't know what to say to her. He'd offered all the support and reassurance he could, but it couldn't dent her fears about her father.

Jamie was with them, too, similarly grave. Only Mayner was still spritely.

"So we're still going to the woods tomorrow night, yeah?" Mayner piped up suddenly. "More reason now than ever."

"I guess we are," Jamie said. "You still wanna go, you two?"

"Wouldn't miss it," replied Kayleigh, managing a brave smile.

"I dunno," said Wren. He looked at Kayleigh. "You sure you're up to it?"

"Don't be daft, I'm fine," she said, bopping him on the shoulder. After a few moments of his sceptical gaze, she grinned and said: "Really, Wren. I'm fine."

"Now you *have* to come," Mayner said over his shoulder to Wren, with a slight note of triumph in his voice.

"I am *so* there," said Wren decisively, punching the air in exaggerated enthusiasm. Truth be told, he was glad to be going; their Friday night excursions had become the stuff of legend, and he rarely failed to enjoy them.

The quiet road that they were following forked ahead, one route heading uphill through a narrow, shady lane, the other curving left and down.

"Well, this is me," said Jamie. "I'll see you guys later. Gimme a call or something."

"'Kay. See ya," Wren replied, and Jamie gave a swift glance either way up the road before crossing to the other side and taking the downward route.

They walked into the dappled shade of the lane, which was barely wide enough for two cars to squeeze past each other and had a pavement on only one side. Clouds of gnats hung in the air, and heavy bees cruised around them on their endless quest for pollen. Out of the direct sun, it became cosily warm, and Wren felt like he could easily go back to sleep again if he stopped walking.

"You spend two-thirds of your life asleep," said Kayleigh, when he told her so. "You must have some cat in you somewhere."

"I don't have a cat in me anywhere," Wren replied. Mayner cackled and made a snap with his fingers.

"You know what I mean," Kayleigh replied, narrowing her eyes in mock-annoyance and wrinkling her nose. Her cutesy expressions seemed a little forced today, but it didn't make them any less cute.

"I don't sleep *that* much," Wren protested.

Mayner choked in front of them at the enormity of this particular lie. "Mate, you are never *awake*. How many times have I called you at, what, three in the afternoon and your mam's had to wake you up? If you didn't have school during the week you wouldn't never see the sun at all. You'd be all pasty-faced with big, round white bug-eyes 'n' shit."

Kayleigh couldn't help laughing at the image.

"I need that much sleep to achieve Buddha-like serenity during my waking hours," Wren replied blandly.

"Oh yeah, you pull *that* off," said Mayner sarcastically. "How wound up do you get when you and Kayleigh argue?"

"Of course *she* winds me up," Wren replied. "She's my girlfriend."

"Hel*lo*, girlfriend within earshot," Kayleigh announced, stepping on his toe.

"You hear something?" Wren asked Mayner, his brow creasing in puzzlement as he looked around.

"Not me," said Mayner, shrugging.

"I'm gonna get you guys for this," Kayleigh promised, and was surprised to find that she had cheered up a little.

They took a right up a set of stone steps with an old iron railing down the centre, into an alley that ran between two tall Victorian buildings that nudged in close on either side. Wren slowed unconsciously as he reached the top of the steps, the humour draining out of him. Kayleigh did the same.

Slouching at the end of the alley were six lads in their late teens and early twenties. Most of them were dressed in sports gear, tracksuits and basketball shoes and the like, but a couple had beige slacks and expensive, top-label shirts. As far as Wren was concerned, either uniform meant the potential for trouble. And they'd come across these guys not a few times before.

Mayner hopped up the stairs after them, but he didn't hesitate for a moment as he saw what was ahead. His face hardened a little, the smile dropping off it, but he carried right on walking. Wren and Kayleigh had no choice but to walk with him.

The lads watched them as they neared, making it plain that they were expected. Wren felt his body go cold with adrenalin. There was a nauseating inevitability about what was to happen. And, as always, it was going to happen to Mayner.

Mayner had always been picked on at school, due to his size and baby-face more than anything. When he had been smaller, he had been shy and introverted because of it, but as time went on things changed around. He began to compensate for his low self-esteem by being relentlessly cheeky to those who tried to bring him down. It worked to an extent – it brought him out of his shell and made him more popular with his classmates, who appreciated his courage; but unfortunately it only made potential bullies hate him all the more. It was a point of pride with him that he would not let anyone extract any satisfaction out of beating him, so they kept on doing it precisely because of that reason. They wanted what little satisfaction they could get, and he was cheating them, and they despised him for it.

"Alright, how's it going?" Mayner said cheerfully to the gang as he reached them.

They didn't reply. Just leaned back against either side of the alley, their cold eyes tracking Mayner and his friends. They would have to walk between the lads to get by, surround themselves if they wanted to pass. Wren felt himself growing angry that he should be put in this position, angry that Kayleigh should have to be exposed to it. No one hated violence more than she did.

Then they were running the gauntlet, mere

centimetres from having to brush up against the lads on either side. Wren kept his eyes ahead, knowing that to meet their gaze would be interpreted as a challenge, but refusing to lower them. Bastards. If he met any of them one-on-one, he'd batter the living shit out of them, assuming Kayleigh wasn't around to see. But they always appeared in number, in a different place each time, meaning that any journey carried a risk of running into them. He'd been with Mayner twice now when these guys had caught him. How many times had he been got and not spoken about it?

And they were past. Wren almost allowed himself to relax in relief. This time they weren't in the mood for it. They were just—

The thought fell incomplete as he felt his arms grabbed and roughly yanked behind him. He heard a cry and saw two of the younger lads restraining Kayleigh in the same way. Two more of them rushed by and pounced on Mayner, throwing him to the path.

Wren thrashed in the grip of those that held him, stamping into the shin of one of them with a satisfyingly painful thud. He was rewarded with a rabbit-punch in the kidneys which numbed his leg and one side of his back. Kayleigh yelped in alarm, swearing like a trooper at their assailants. But she knew as well as Wren did that the lads were just keeping them from interfering in business, and their business was with Mayner.

"Whoa, clumsy," said Mayner, getting up with a sheepish grin on his face. "I guess I tripped."

A greasy-skinned twenty-year-old in Nikes and a

white tracksuit slapped him hard around the head as he was clambering to his feet, sending him down again. "So did I," he commented, following it up with a kick in the ribs that lifted Mayner a couple of inches off the ground.

"You shiteaters!" Wren shouted, roused to fury. "Takes two of you to kick in a kid half your size? You take on grandmothers for an encore?"

One of the lads who held him back suddenly twisted him into an armlock, a clumsy attempt at copying what he had seen on police dramas. It was painful enough to make Wren grit his teeth and yell through them. Kayleigh struggled against her captors, calling his name, but it only made him feel more helpless.

Mayner got up again, coughing, and looked Tracksuit in the eyes. "Please sir, may I have some more?" he said.

This time it was beige slacks and powder-blue shirt who responded, punching him dead in the spine and making him collapse again, then following it up – for want of anything more original to do – by kicking him in the ribs again.

Once more, Mayner pulled himself up, smiled, and said, "Are you guys gonna get on with it or what? I've got an appointment with the hairdresser at five."

Wren winced away at the series of thuds that followed. Unable to look at what they were doing to his friend, he instead made a quick mental head-count of those around him. Two with him, two with Kayleigh; all about his age or younger. And the two older ones, the obvious ringleaders: Tracksuit and Slacks. They didn't need or deserve names, even if Wren had known them. Their

23

faces were forgettable, cut from the same production mould as a million of their comrades.

An absurdly funny thought occurred to him then, that if he looked on the soles of their feet he might find a serial number followed by their brand name, like an action figure. 3BXX45 THUG, or something.

Mayner doggedly refused to make a noise as they slapped and punched and kicked him, never really damaging him, just humiliating him and causing him pain. The moment the barrage stopped, Mayner would say: "Is that it?" or "What's that supposed to be? I've had better kickings at playschool," and so on. He knew full well it would only get him a further beating, but he wouldn't let it rest. Then, finally, when the bruises on his jaw and around one eye were already beginning to darken and swell, he looked levelly at Tracksuit and said, very carefully and thoughtfully: "You know, I think your mother could quite possibly be a filthy, scabby whore."

"Mayner, will you *shut up*?" Kayleigh cried in alarm.

"Oh, that's it," Tracksuit grated, in a tone that said his playing around had suddenly turned serious. "I've had *enough* of your mouth."

But instead of delivering another series of blows, he leaned down near to Mayner and said: "Next time we meet, you puny shit, I'm gonna beat you raw, and I'm not gonna stop till something breaks."

Mayner began to reply, but was cut short by a parting kick in the belly that knocked the wind out of him. The others released Wren and Kayleigh and walked away to join Tracksuit and Slacks, and the six of them wandered off down the alley.

Wren and Kayleigh ran over to Mayner and helped him up. Wren was physically shaking with rage. He hated being made to feel so inadequate, so useless. He hated being unable to defend his friend. He should have turned round and attacked them the minute they let him loose, no matter how futile it would have been; that he had done nothing made him a coward. He felt like a chickenshit in front of his girlfriend, even though he knew that she would despise him if he had fought them. And he knew that however badly he felt, Mayner was feeling a hundred times worse.

He didn't believe anyone on Earth deserved to die, but if he ever changed his mind, he knew that people like them would be first in line.

"Mayner? You okay?" Wren asked, as his friend wiped the back of his hand across his bloody lips.

"Just fine," he replied, his gaze following the retreating bunch, hard and dull as a rusted knife. "Those bastards are gonna get theirs."

"Don't, please," said Kayleigh. "It'll only make things worse."

Mayner didn't reply, just carried on watching them as a cat watches a grounded flock of birds in its yard.

Mayner didn't want to walk with them any more that day. It was clear that he was ashamed of what had happened to him, and didn't want their sympathy, so they let him go off on an alternative route back to his house. They resumed their journey through the perfect sunshine, talking little. The combined effect of the head's announcement, Kayleigh's subdued mood and

Mayner's beating had killed any attempt to muster good spirits, even on such a glorious day. When they kissed their parting, at the junction near their houses, it was more because it was expected than because of any real passion. Weighed down, they left each other, and Wren made the last leg of his journey alone.

His feet took him down a route so familiar that he didn't have to think about navigation, leaving his mind free to wander. War? Were they really heading into a war? Was it possible? He'd often been accused of concerning himself with issues that a seventeen-year-old shouldn't worry about. Where his classmates and friends watched TV in the evenings, he would satisfy his relentless thirst for knowledge by reading. As Mayner had commented before, he did appear over-educated, at least by the standards of his age. That was half the reason why he dressed like a skater, whom most of the adult population assumed were either thick or chronic miscreants. It kind of evened things out.

He was also unfailingly cynical, as the one thing his endeavours had taught him was that nothing ever worked, politics were useless, and almost every major catastrophe or near-catastrophe that man had caused had been through idiocy that a four-year-old could have avoided. That was one point that he and Kayleigh agreed on, and in fact one of the reasons he had first been attracted to her. She was a dedicated pacifist, and he knew how utterly stupid war was.

But all the thinking he had done about it, all the ideas and information he had absorbed, had never prepared him for the possibility that it might really *happen*. For the briefest of moments, he caught a glimpse of the enormity of the events that were occurring around him, and it was a terrifying wave that threatened to overwhelm him. He shut it out, afraid. Think about it later.

It was while searching for something else to catch his interest, needing the distraction, that he chanced to look in through the window of a record store as he was passing and didn't see the girl coming out of the door just in front of him. They bumped heavily into each other, and he instinctively caught her by the arm as she fell with an exclamation of shock.

"My fault, sorry," he said automatically. "You're alright?"

The girl straightened, and recognition dawned in his eyes, followed by an almost tangible clutch of some emotion that he didn't even have a name for.

She was a little smaller than him, but the extra inch or two was made up by the blue Independent beanie she wore. A black Rainer Maria T-shirt fell loose over a pair of outsize Droors, and she had a pack on her back of the same kind as Wren's. Her face was beautifully formed, a slight coffee-cream colour to her complexion evidence of her Anglo-Japanese parentage, and her hair was so black that it seemed to absorb the light around it.

For a moment, he was too surprised to say anything; but a moment was all it took. He knew her expressions better than anyone; she had been about to tell him it was okay, no harm done, and genuinely mean it because she was forgiving like that. But as she registered who it was standing before her, she closed up like a fan and her face and gaze grew chill. She swept past him without a sound, adjusting the pack on her shoulders, dismissing him.

He stood there outside the record store for a time, leaning against the window and looking up at the clear azure sky, before the owner came out and asked him to move.

CHAPTER THREE

"Keeping you updated on the movements in the Far East, here's Leslie Crane. Leslie, that looks like a weather map you have there."

"Ha, yes, I suppose you could say that. This is a diagram of the forces accumulating in the Far East. As you can see, there's certainly a lot of activity. These arrows represent the path of advance of each faction, and these circles are where forces have built up and are static. Over here we have the long, curved lines where the Russian Federation navy have come east of Japan and south to the Philippines. Here, where this circle is, Chinese and Mongolian ground troops have massed on Vietnam's northern border. West of Indonesia, the Kazakhstan navy have been on manoeuvres in the Indian Ocean, and have accumulated quite a sizeable amount of ships.

"This is the situation as it stood yesterday. Since then, the navies have continued their sweep through the island chain that comprises Indonesia, the Philippines, Papua New Guinea and Malaysia. You can see here how they have moved on from the Philippines, pushing past Palau to assault the northern coasts of Indonesia, and here to the west also, on the Malaysian coast. China and Mongolia as yet have made no move south into Vietnam and Laos, but the heavy troop presence on the border has caused a great deal of friction. The navy of Kazakhstan has also begun to sweep across the Indian Ocean, westward towards Kenya and Somalia.

"It certainly seems that the armies of the Eastern Alliance are following the predicted pattern of invasion put forward by German General Hans Kempfner several days ago. They seem intent on acquiring countries along the equator, but factors such as economic wealth or natural resources apparently matter little to the members of the Eastern Alliance. The question now, as always, is why?"

Wren had never felt an atmosphere such as the one he found at Sacred Heart the next day. Even after one of their former pupils, Danny Crane, had been run over and killed by a Merc while crossing the road at the treacherous bus lay-by, the school had never been as subdued as this. Then, it had only directly affected the tiny proportion of pupils who were his friends; Wren had grimly reflected that there was a great gap between those who genuinely grieved, and those who thought they *should* grieve so as to prove they had a soul.

But now it was different. Now it was something else. A dark pall had settled on the school like a thick velvet blanket; and even when somebody laughed, it seemed a little too loud and they trailed off into nervous embarrassment. Usually, the closed-off world of secondary education was the perfect remedy to worrying about the bigger picture, but today it seemed that everyone wore a little more care than usual.

It started with another special assembly, this time during the first period of the day. Mr Renford explained that some leaflets would be handed around the classes during the day, and that some of the teachers would be drilling the pupils in some basic safety techniques. Leaving the exact details unclear, he then urged everyone not be alarmed by these measures, which of course had precisely the opposite effect. Renford had the air of a man who knew that whatever he did would be wrong, so he had squared his gunbelt and got on with it.

"Now, I don't really know how to go about telling you this," said Miss Urquhart in second-period English, "but I'm required by the government to pass out these information packs. They arrived special delivery this morning. Please don't be worried about their contents, they're for a worst-case scenario only. And I mean the very worst case."

A gabble spread over the class as the small, thin booklets were passed from left to right. One girl started crying. When they reached Wren, he nearly laughed; but the laugh was more surprise than humour. It was just not the first thing you expected to fall into your hands in second-period English. *Survival in the Event of a Nuclear Strike.*

"I expect this may all seem very frightening to you," said Miss Urquhart. She was young and willowy, not unattractive, soft-voiced and kinder than most teachers. It made her the subject of many half-formed fantasies in the lower years, if only they could get over the fact that her name sounded like someone burping and being sick at the same time. "But really, it's just a precaution. I can't stress that enough. Whenever two countries with full nuclear capability go to war, the government insists we hand these out."

"And how many times has *that* happened?" Wren said, loud enough for everyone to hear.

Miss Urquhart didn't answer him, just shot him a look of vague disdain meaning: *I am the authority here, you are nothing.* It reassured the pupils while neatly sidestepping the fact that Wren was right, it *had* never happened, and they'd never had to deal with anything like this before in her lifetime.

Wren took off his cap to rub his fingertips across his sweaty scalp – which was prickling in the heat of the classroom – and replaced it again, the peak shading his nape against the sun's beams that streamed through the windows. He tugged his T-shirt out at the shoulders, where it was sticking with sweat, and leafed through the booklet while Miss Urquhart babbled instructions she knew nothing about in the background.

The information was presented in a no-nonsense manner, without avoiding any of the gory details about what might happen if you *didn't* follow the instructions within. Obviously it had not been intended for children. Wren could imagine the first years having spontaneous nervous breakdowns reading it. All the usual stuff about fall-out, radiation poisoning, how to build and stock your own shelter (in a week? He'd like to see *that*) and so on and so forth. There was nothing there he hadn't already read about elsewhere, and he lost interest after a time and began looking out of the window again. It was odd; he felt that he *should* be alarmed about it all, but he couldn't bring himself to actually feel that way. The governments were just showing off; it wouldn't come to war. Probably.

Or if he was really honest, it was just that he was denying it to himself. The possibility of nuclear conflict was too big and too damn scary to even consider.

The classroom where his English lessons were held looked out across the playing fields, with one of the bus lay-bys beyond where most of the children went to catch their ride home at the end of the day. It was also one of the only legitimate exits from the school – excluding hedges and so on, when leaving undetected was the key – and so it was frequently trafficked by sixth-formers who had free periods and were off to the park or down the vil. On a scorching day like this, Wren was not surprised to see a good few on their way already.

He frowned a little as something caught his eye. Just by the entrance, a group of figures were standing. For a moment, he thought they might be Tracksuit and Slacks and the rest of those guys, but even though his long-range vision had never been very good, he could tell by the out-of-focus blur of their clothes that it wasn't them.

Most of them wore tight jeans – looking uncomfortably tight to someone who was used to wearing clothes four sizes too big – and had black bomber jackets. Some had short-cropped hair, some had skinheads. That was about as much as he could make out. He saw them hand something to a pair of sixth-formers as they passed, and the pupils stopped and talked for a few moments before leaving.

"Andrew Wren?" Miss Urquhart called, snapping his mind back to the classroom. "I suppose you think you know enough about what's in this book to afford to ignore it and look out of the window?"

"I know it's basically regurgitating the information provided in the British government pamphlet *Protect and Survive*, which tells you how to make a fall-out shelter in your home using mattresses and doors leaned up against walls, and to stockpile food and water so you don't have to go outside for fourteen days while the fall-out loses its potency, and a bunch of other crap that is basically there to prolong your life for enough time to enjoy the diseased mess that's left of the world before you starve to death or drink poisoned water or cut your foot and get gangrene and die horribly 'cause there's no medicine."

Some of the class laughed. Miss Urquhart smiled, accepting his answer with good grace, and looked around the room. "Lovely attitude, Andrew," she said. "Now class, forget what Andrew just said and carry on."

There was another ripple of laughter, and the tension in the class eased for a precious few minutes.

*

The day dragged on without any of the usual troubles. Teachers knew it was near-impossible to get pupils to concentrate towards the end of a Friday; they were all tired from the long week and restless to start the weekend. Today, it made no difference. Nobody had their minds on lessons all day, not even the teachers. They sauntered in fifteen minutes late for class, set a few exercises which nobody bothered to do, and left again. Only a few hardliners saw it as their citizen's duty to keep discipline, and were especially rigid on the slacking pupils.

When the final bell rang, there was none of the relief or excitement that it usually provoked. Pupils sloped out of the school, their minds already on the news broadcasts that would be reported to them by their parents when they got home.

Kayleigh and Jamie had not come in today; but Mayner had, surprisingly, so he and Wren met up as they walked out of the school and up the drive to leave the grounds.

"Glad to get out of there," Mayner said. His bruises had faded to discoloured smudges now, and his split lip had a fat scab on it. "Like a bloody mortuary all day."

"Yeah, well, grim warnings about nuclear extinction tend to dampen the public a bit."

"Not you, too?" Mayner asked with a groan.

"Nah, I'm not too bothered," Wren said, cocking a cheek thoughtfully. "It's not gonna happen. It's not even worth worrying about. They always back off at the last minute, whether it's war or politics. Nothing ever gets done. Nobody's decisive enough to start a proper war."

He hoped he was really as convinced as he sounded.

Mayner shucked his pack up on his shoulders. The straps were chafing against his sweat-moistened underarms. "Thought you were gonna go gloomy on me then," he said.

"Been thinking," Wren replied. "I bumped into Cass yesterday."

"Ex-girlfriend Cass?"

"Know any others?"

"Yeah, Cass who works at the café. And my cousin Cass."

Wren's comeback having been shot down in flames, he did his best to make a recovery. "Well, neither of them. Ex-girlfriend Cass."

"You talk to her?"

Wren squinted up at the sky. "I think she'd probably have killed me."

"Still like that, huh?"

"Still like that."

"You ever talked to her since . . . y'know?"

Wren shrugged. "We never talked about it. Not even . . . not even while we were still together. After it happened."

"Been over a year. Eighteen months, is it?"

"For God's sake, Mayner," Wren exclaimed, then turned to look at his friend. "What would I say? Put yourself in my place. How am I supposed to begin?"

Mayner rubbed an imaginary fleck of dirt off the back of his hand. "It's not like it was your fault, was it?"

"Depends on your point of view. As far as Cass is concerned, it was *all* my fault."

"You don't know that."

"Yeah, I do," Wren replied, and that was the end of it.

Mayner pulled out a tab and fired it, deliberately doing it while still on school grounds to make a statement that the teachers held no power over him. He took a drag, blew out and then gestured with the two fingers that held the cigarette. "So who are *those* guys?"

It was the group that Wren had observed earlier, during second-period English and Holocaust Survival. He had noticed they had disappeared and reappeared throughout the day, but he had never been able to see what they were doing. At first he suspected drugs, but they were being far too obvious for that. They were standing to either side of the gate through which the pupils had to walk, and as Wren and Mayner approached it was possible to see what they were doing. Pamphlets, that was all. They were handing out pamphlets.

He hadn't intended to take one. To be honest, he didn't much like the look of the people handing them out. They were all mid-twenties, exclusively male, and they had a slightly edgy look about them. Not edgy in a nervous way, more in psychotic vein. He had no doubt that these were people to whom you did not give any shit. Plus their clothing and hair – or lack of it – gave them an uncomfortably fascist look, although Wren knew that plenty of other social groups wore similar clothes and it was often difficult to tell them apart.

But Mayner – who had probably thought exactly the same thing about them being dangerous – had walked over to one of them. His nature did not allow him to even entertain the thought of being afraid of anyone, and so the very fact that he thought they looked nasty was enough to spur him to go get a flyer to prove to himself that he wasn't scared.

"Alright, mate," he said as he approached one of them, a pinch-faced man with a strong, narrow beak of a nose and a skinhead.

"Alright. 'Ow are ya?" His eyes flickered over Mayner's bruises.

"I'm good. What's all this?" Mayner asked, taking one of the proffered pamphlets. Wren came over to stand next to him and look over his shoulder.

"You 'ave one too, mate," said the skinhead, giving one to Wren.

He glanced at the cover. It was printed in black ink on cheap saffron-yellow paper, a Union Jack wrapped around a pair of AK-47 assault rifles. Beneath it was stamped in stencil-type letters: "UKCDF: UNITED KINGDOM CITIZEN'S DEFENCE FORCE MANIFESTO".

Wren blinked. A militant nationalist group. Didn't get them coming out of the woodwork very often.

"You gonna be ready to defend your country when the time comes? Read it," the skinhead said, tapping the pamphlet with his index finger.

"I will," Wren lied, and pocketed it. Mayner did the same.

"Later," he said cheerily.

"See ya," said the skinhead, already turning to distribute more pamphlets.

*

Jamie stood against the breakfast bar of his kitchen, sipping a cup of coffee absently and listening to the radio. It had an almost mesmerizing quality to it. The last thing he wanted to know was how the invasion was progressing and the international reaction to it. He wanted to just forget it was all happening. But all day, he kept on finding himself back, again and again, drawn to the radio like a crowd to a car crash.

He'd not really had any idea what he was going to do today, only that he couldn't face school. So he'd lain about the house, watching trash television or idly wandering through a first-person RPG on his PC. Nothing had captured him. Most of the stuff on telly was either directly or obliquely to do with war anyway. The three-week build-up since tensions began had given the schedulers plenty of time to line up a slew of old programmes on various conflicts over the last few years.

It was one of those documentaries about World War Two that caught him and got him thinking. An annoying blend of cheap computer graphics and old black-and-white footage from the time. Factsheets kept on coming up over the scenes of destroyed sections of London and bombers howling around in the sky. It was called *The War at Home*, and despite all the shots of out-and-out warfare, it was basically about the effect that the war had on the English public. Rationing, blackouts, air-raid sirens and barrage balloons floating over everything like eerie sentries in the night. Facts were spewed out at him, not really penetrating. Something daft like more people in British cities were killed in car crashes than by

German bombs because they had to cover their headlights in the blackouts, or similar.

And then there was a shot of the conscription line, where the young men queued – willingly or otherwise – to await their turn to be processed. It struck him like a hammer in the chest, suddenly. One man in particular, turning to face the camera, a look of utter resignation on his face. It reminded him of footage he'd seen of Eastern European countries in starvation. The way he had given himself up to his fate. He was going to war, and nothing he could do would change it.

That's me, Jamie thought, and a sudden horror grabbed him and refused to let him go.

For the rest of the day he thought about it, feeling the terrible inevitability slowly crush him as he came to one dead-end solution after another. It was his eighteenth birthday in less than three weeks; he was the eldest of their group of friends by some months.

Eighteen. Draft age.

The facts didn't really matter. He wasn't sure if they had drafted boys as young as sixteen in the World Wars, or what the procedure was now, over fifty years on. But he had become fixated on the prospect of his eighteenth birthday, the traditional turnpike between being a child and manhood.

There's gonna be a war, and they're gonna make me fight in it.

He couldn't remember a more sickening feeling of powerlessness than he experienced then. He imagined it was like an innocent man being told he was to be sent to a violent jail for ten years; the sense that someone else had taken the control of his life out of his hands, and was dictating what should happen to him. The more he thought and obsessed, the more he worked himself into a tighter and tighter knot, until by the time his father returned home from work, he felt like he was only barely holding together.

Jamie's father, Perry, was a military man by nature. He walked with a stiff, upright bearing. His hair was short and neat and he kept an orderly ginger moustache. His eyes were a weathered green, the colour of combat slacks, and he ran his house like a barracks. But he was not a soldier, not any more.

Once, he and Kayleigh's father had trained in the same unit; but after only three years in the service, he suffered a knee injury that crippled him for six months and would never heal properly again. He was not qualified for any other post except as an infantryman, and being physically impaired wrote that particular vocation off. Somewhere in the bureaucratic mess of the army administration, he slipped through the net and was given an honourable discharge against his will. Few were more dedicated to the lifestyle of the Forces than he was, and when they betrayed him by letting him go, it broke his heart. He returned to civilian life and became an office clerk; but he never gave up the old army routines.

Jamie sat in his room and listened as the front door shut and Perry began to make himself tea in the kitchen. He knew it was a mistake to talk to his father about this, but he needed something to calm the whirl of thoughts in his head, and whatever advice or opinion Perry offered was certain to be stable and forthright. Even if it was bad – which he was fairly sure it would be – he would have something definite to pin the rest of his fears to and stop them flapping around like ribbons in a cyclone.

Perry was sitting at the table when Jamie came in, reading the paper with his mug of tea on a coaster next to him. He looked up briefly as his son sat down, then returned his gaze to the paper. For a few moments, Jamie watched him, his hands fiddling anxiously beneath the table. His father ignored him.

"Did you hear about the Eastern Alliance invading Indonesia now?" Jamie began. He already knew the answer, but it was something to say.

"Hmm," his father said, not looking up. "Quite a mess."

"What do you think's going to happen?"

Perry sipped his tea. "I think we ought to bloody well kick them out," he said. "Not that I give a monkey's about those little islands, but you can't have the Soviets just snapping up countries willy-nilly."

Jamie wasn't even sure that *Soviets* applied to Russia any more, but he didn't query it.

"You think we should go to war?"

"I think we *will* go to war."

"Oh."

Silence. Perry rustled his paper, smoothing out a kink in the tiny column text.

"What'll happen then?"

His father gave him a look, as if to say: *you really expect me to answer?*

"No, I mean, you think it'll be limited warfare like with the Falklands? Or the Gulf War? Keep the fighting over there?"

"I really don't know," Perry said, sighing. He just wanted Jamie to go away and stop plaguing him with questions.

Realizing that his father was not going to cooperate with his attempts at beat around-the-bush, he decided to be a little more direct.

"If there *is* a war, like a proper one," he said, "you think they'll introduce conscription?"

Perry put down the paper with a tut of irritation and looked at his son. He had never been a man who had been particularly interested in feelings – including his own – and the fact that Jamie was desperately worried passed him by completely. For some unfathomable reason, his son was annoying him with inane conversation, and he wanted to get it over with so he could get back to reading his paper.

"If there *is* full-scale conflict, then conscription may well become necessary. But you needn't worry about that. The government always ask for volunteers before they introduce conscription, and I should make bloody sure that you sign up when your country calls for you."

Jamie looked like a scared rabbit.

"If there's one thing I can't stand," he continued, "it's these moaning lefties who take what the country has to give them and then refuse to give her anything back. Britain cares for us, and we owe her a debt, so I won't allow you to shirk your responsibility to your country. And you can bet I'll be signing up the first chance I get."

Of course, Jamie thought. He should have expected it. His father actually *wanted* a war, because his years of military training would make him valuable to the army. The army could afford to be choosy in peacetime, but if it came to a World War then they would need every hand they could get, and a little thing like a trick knee would not be a problem any more. Perry would get his wish, to be back in the service. Unfortunately, he'd drag his son with him.

Jamie just sat there for a few moments. After a time, seeing that his son did not have anything else to say, Perry picked up his paper and put it up in front of his face like a barrier.

The phone rang. Jamie went to get it. It was Mayner.

CHAPTER FOUR

"With us in the studio is Jeffrey Gail, political correspondent for the London Herald. Mr Gail, good evening."

"Good evening."

"Mr Gail, do you think it was really wise for NATO to declare this morning that they would be holding an emergency announcement to the press tonight – at nine o'clock pm Greenwich Mean Time – and then leave the media to speculate wildly throughout the day? Doesn't that run counter to what they have been trying to do ever since this crisis began: keeping the public calm and panic to a minimum?"

"Absolutely, I think it was terribly unwise of them to make such an apparently rash move. Absolutely. But that in itself tells a story. NATO knew exactly what effect their action would have. It is possible they did this intentionally, and having the press . . . riled up, if you *will, is what they want. I can't imagine what the purpose of this would be, but of course we are basically working in the dark here until NATO decide to let go of what they know."*

"And do you think that this announcement will be the answer to all our questions?"

"I should hope so, I really should. I think NATO have treated the public shockingly. I am under no illusions at all that they know exactly why the Eastern Alliance have suddenly become so aggressive. They're not telling us, that's all. But there's another, and more likely reason for making such a declaration. They were backed into a corner. My guess is that someone threatened to go public with whatever information NATO have been holding back, and demanded that either NATO make the public aware of it, or they themselves would. NATO declared the press meeting immediately, and they have the day to debate how best to present their revelations."

"You really think it will be as important as that? Don't you think this may be a storm over nothing?"

"Oh, I'm positive. I'd stake my reputation on the fact that whatever NATO has to tell us, it is going to be very interesting."

A twig cracked, and Mayner knew the game was up. Before anyone could react, he jumped out of the darkness between the trees, making a low "boogadaboogada" noise which sounded so ridiculous that Kayleigh, far from being frightened, started laughing uncontrollably until she retched.

Mayner was worryingly hyperactive tonight,

overflowing with energy. Jamie, by contrast, was very subdued, and had hardly said a word to anyone, making Wren wonder why he had come out at all if he was feeling so down. But here he was, pack on his back, walking with them through the woods under a darkening sky. The moon was full and high, even though the sun had not yet given up the battlefield.

Maybe it was habit that brought him. The Friday night excursions were held only once a month, and it had become a cardinal sin to miss one. Wren's dad shuttled them all out into the countryside that surrounded Sheffield, they found a piece of woodland that looked promising, and then he left them there till morning with their tents and food, firewood and alcohol – and his mobile phone "just in case". Wren had come to love these trips, for it was the one time when they could get away from parents, schoolwork and other distractions and just shoot the shit for a while. The combination of the woodland venue, the campfire and the inevitable drunkenness always fired a philosophical spark in them, and Wren had come across more profound insights on his Friday night excursions than in much of the literature he had read.

He knew what tonight's topic of conversation would be. No matter how much they steered around it, the prospect of war would rear its head. In fact, Kayleigh had even brought a radio, tuned to the BBC World Service, to keep abreast of the developments. Wren had thought about protesting, that it would ruin the point of the excursion, but he didn't have the heart. He could see that beneath her controlled exterior she was becoming more and more frantic about her father.

It was a small wood that they had chosen this time, probably not even a mile from one uneven end to the other. The trees grew sparsely, with knee-high underbrush in between and time-worn rambling paths snaking through the gaps. It was dusk, the sun not fully set even at eight o'clock, and the air was pleasantly dry and warm. A soft breeze rustled the trees, setting up a ghostly hiss as they shivered their limbs. There were few forest noises, for the birds had fallen silent and the insects were tuning up at home, and peace was all around them.

"You brought the firelighters this time, didn't you?" Mayner asked Wren, while they waited for Kayleigh to catch her breath after her mirth-spasm.

"The wood was *wet*. It wasn't that we had no firelighters," Wren replied.

"But if we'd had firelighters, we might not have taken three hours to get it going, right?"

"If you hadn't fallen in that brook, we'd have had dry wood and wouldn't have *needed* firelighters."

"Hmm," Mayner replied, seeing that he was defeated.

"We'd better stop soon," Kayleigh said, squeezing Wren's hand. "We're gonna walk out of the other side of these trees if we keep going."

"There's a bit of a clearing over there," Jamie said, his voice unusually dull and toneless. He wasn't even looking, just wiping the lenses of his spectacles with a handkerchief.

"Where?" said Mayner. "Oh, that. You wanna stop?"

He was asking everyone in general.

"It's quite small," Kayleigh said.

"It's big enough," said Wren, careful not to say anything that might discourage Jamie from speaking again.

"Let's go check it out, at least," Mayner said, bounding off into the darkness before anyone could stop him.

The clearing was wider than it first appeared, and they had pitched their Eurohike bubble-tents within a few minutes. Kayleigh and Wren were sharing, and so were Jamie and Mayner, though Mayner didn't seem too happy at the prospect with the mood Jamie was in. Eventually, they settled, and Kayleigh – being the premier pyro among them – set to work on the fire, unpacking the wood that they had brought. The radio was brought out and droned in the background, kept at a low volume so that it was not intruding on their conversation. Wren distributed cans of Amstel – their latest discovery in the highly selective field of lager drinking – and the silent woods were treated to the crack and hiss of several cans being pulled, and then the yelp as one of them blew up in a spray of foam.

"Funny," said Mayner flatly, his face dripping as Wren cackled with glee. Every bag of alcohol had the obligatory beer bomb hidden in it somewhere; it was another dumb custom that had grown up around the Friday night legend.

"You guys are such a bunch of jocks," Kayleigh commented, pausing in the construction of a pyramid of wood for the fire.

"Which makes you a jock's girlfriend," Wren replied.

"Ugh. That's worse, isn't it?"

"Much."

"Okay, you're not jocks. Until I dump you."

The fire got going and the Amstel supply began to disappear, the cans finding their way into a rubbish bag that they'd brought with them. Kayleigh wouldn't have them leaving any mess when they camped, and even insisted Mayner dropped his butts in an empty beer can to take home with them. It was all part of the routine by now.

Eventually, sitting around the newly emerging fire as the last light fled the sky, Mayner took advantage of a lull in the conversation to introduce the topic that they had all been thinking about.

"So, what you gonna do if the bomb drops?"

Jamie, who had taken only a cursory part in the proceedings until then, looked up suddenly.

"*May*ner. . ." Kayleigh said.

"Well, y'know, it's something you gotta think about, really. Let's not beat around the bush here, we might be facing a nuclear war if the Americans and Russians go at it."

"That's a little grim," Wren said.

"Come on, as if *you* haven't thought of it," Mayner accused, then settled back with a distant smile on his face. "As for me, when the nukes drop, I'm gonna sit on my roof in a deckchair, wearing swimming trunks and sunglasses. If I'm going out, I'm going out with a tan."

"You think Sheffield's got any kind of civil defence

programme?" Kayleigh asked. "Like shelters and stuff? Underground bunkers?"

Wren snorted. "Doubt it. Back in 1980 this guy Belstead was head of civil defence at the Home Office, and he reckoned it would take sixty thousand *million* pounds to provide proper blast and fall-out shelters for the British people. Four years after that, the total civil defence budget was only sixty-seven million. Little bit of a shortfall."

"You know *far* too much," Kayleigh said, poking him.

"It's a depressing way to be. I'd rather be ignorant, it's easier to be content."

"Poor baby."

"Poor me."

"It's not gonna be nuclear," said Jamie suddenly, drawing in the dirt between his feet with a twig. They turned to look at him, surprised by the certainty in his voice. "Nobody'd dare fire off their missiles. They know they'd get blown to pieces in the retaliation strike. Nobody's that crazy."

"So what do you reckon, Jamie?" Wren asked, coaxing him out of his shell.

"It'll be like in the Gulf, but everywhere," he said, and there was an oddly emotionless cast to his voice. "Smart bombs, computer-guided missiles, all that stuff. And troops. Loads of troops, like in the Falklands or something. We'll have to fight them off the Philippines, and whatever. Maybe we'll go full-on, like a proper world war. But nobody's stupid enough to use a nuke. The minute one country fired, every other country would, and in four hours the Earth is a cinder."

"Uhh . . . hate to burst your bubble, Jamie, but the human race *is* full of very stupid people," said Kayleigh. Wren laid a hand on her arm and gave her a glance that said: *leave it.* If Kayleigh got on to one of her rants, Jamie would just give up talking, and he'd never find out what was bothering his friend.

"No, but think about it," Jamie said, suddenly animate, the meagre firelight catching the lenses of his glasses as if his eyes had burst into flame. He appeared to have not even heard Kayleigh's comment. "Two days ago, everything was just normal, we were just . . . life was just . . . I dunno. I could look into the future, ten years from now, and I'd be like 'Oh, I might have *this* job or be living in *this* city', but things would still be . . . y'know, *safe.* It'd be under *my* control. You get it?"

"I think so," Wren said, before Mayner could reply in negative.

"But this whole war thing, it just makes me realize how much it's all just a big illusion, that I actually have no choice at all in my life. Right now, fat guys in their mid-fifties are deciding whether or not to start a war, not thinking about what it's gonna do to *me* . . . to *us.* You know what happens if we don't get nuked? We get conscripted, or forced to work in factories, and in the meantime our homes get bombed and blown up by missiles fired from half the world away. And one day, Wren, you're gonna be on the frontline and you're gonna hear how your old mate Mayner, who you haven't seen for years since you were posted in different countries, has been killed by a landmine; or you'll get injured and come home to find your dad was in a building that collapsed in an air raid, or your mam's died of pneumonia 'cause she was too underfed on rations to fight it off. We don't have any *control*! If the PM decides to start a war, he can come knocking on my door and make me go fight and kill in a country I never gave a shit about, he can destroy my life and everything I planned for, and I can't do a damn thing about it!"

Jamie was almost shouting by the time he finished, and the others had lapsed into a slightly stunned silence, looking at him in bewilderment.

"Is that what's been on your mind, Jamie?" Wren asked warily. Jamie was prone to lapsing into depressions, in which he worried himself into the ground. "You have been pretty quiet today."

"Yeah, that's exactly what's been on your mind," his friend replied angrily. "Don't any of you see? Don't *any* of you get what this *means*? If we start a war, our lives are *over*."

"*Get* what this *means*?" Kayleigh exploded suddenly. "My *father* is out there, he could be *dead* for all I know, and you're bleating about how hard it's gonna be for you on the off-chance we do decide to go to war? My father is already *there*, Jamie. The war's already begun for him! You selfish son of a bitch, *he might be dead*! So don't give me all this piteous crap about something that might not even happen; I'm living the damn thing already!"

She jumped to her feet, throwing Wren's arm violently off her, and stalked away from the firelight into the trees, her footsteps crunching away into silence.

Mayner looked slowly from Jamie to Wren. "Shouldn't you go after her?" he asked.

Wren cocked an eyebrow. "You don't know her when she's like this. She'd rather be left alone."

Jamie had retreated back into himself, chastised, drawing in the dirt between his knees again with his head hung.

"You should've said something, mate," Mayner said, putting a hand on Jamie's shoulder.

"What was the point?" he said. "None of us can do anything about it."

"Yeah, but still. . ." Mayner said, inconclusively.

Wren knew what Mayner had missed, however. Jamie was like his father in a lot of ways, as little as he would have liked to admit it. Talking about his problems was a kind of weakness to him; he had been instilled with the belief that a man should deal with his own troubles and not burden anyone else with them. That was a woman's way, his father would have said. And though Jamie himself would never have actually *said* such a thing, he thought it.

He must be really screwed up about it to be telling *us*, Wren thought. Really *badly* screwed up.

He was about to reply when suddenly Jamie held his hand up for silence. He reached over to the radio, that had been droning quietly in the background, and turned it up to conversation level.

". . .*in the wake of the announcement, governments are urging the people of the world not to panic. Experts are saying that the situation can be handled and that the public, or the media, should not make any decisions based on something they know nothing about. But the cry of every voice here is* why? *Why weren't we told sooner? Why was it kept from us, when it was plain that the authorities of both NATO and the Eastern Alliance knew full well the scale of the impending catastrophe?"*

"Is this that nine o'clock NATO announcement everyone was—?" Mayner began, but Wren shushed him, staring intently at the little radio.

". . .become clear that NATO are not willing to deal with the allegation of withholding information from the public, but rather they are concentrating on the matter to hand. Speculation has been made that cooperation against this mutual enemy could bring the war to a sudden close, but this reporter thinks it very unlikely. It has become obvious now that this development will be the cause of the war, not the solution."

"And Peter will be bringing half-hourly reports from Brussels to keep you up to date on the situation there. Now, for those who have tuned in late, only one headline will dominate the news tomorrow, only one story will sit on the front pages. There is an air of . . . disbelief in the studio here, I can tell you, and I'm sure that is echoed all around the world right at this moment. Here, with a recap of the announcement made by NATO only minutes ago, is Lloyd Finnegan."

The three of them listened, the fire snapping between them, unheard. When Kayleigh came back, they were silent, and when Wren looked up at her with a sharp and frightened gaze like a deer caught in the headlights of an oncoming car, she knew that something terrible had happened. In that instant, terror brushed her. World War Three?

She sat down, and they told her, and she realized then that her fears had fallen way short of the mark. It was worse than that. Much worse.

CHAPTER FIVE

"With us in the studio now we have Professor Maliard, arguably the most eminent climatologist in his field, with an impressive array of publications and awards that make him, perhaps, the person most qualified to tell us about what is going on."

"You're too kind."

"Professor, there's only one question that I'm sure everyone wants to ask. How did this happen?"

"Well, you see, you can't approach it with that kind of attitude, you know. You shouldn't sound so surprised. Climatologists have been warning of the possibility of exactly this occurrence for decades now, but it seems that no one wants to know unless there has been some kind of action film made about it with Arnold Schwarzenberger—"

"Schwarzenegger."

"Do forgive me. My point is this: the warnings have

been there for a long time now. It is just that nobody chose to listen. The public are more scared of an asteroid striking the Earth, which would be the equivalent of winning the cosmic National Lottery and then some, and they completely ignore something like this, that was naturally supposed to happen. And so we are unprepared."

"Professor, are you saying that scientists have known about this for—"

"Everyone has known about it. Governments have been told, it is in libraries for all to read, but nobody wants it on the news and nobody wants to deal with it. Now I am afraid we are going to have to."

"But even so, Professor, you said it was 'naturally supposed to happen.'"

"Oh yes. The Earth is not such a hospitable place as recent history would have you believe. The rocks deep in the Earth tell us the real story. This planet spends ninety thousand years out of every hundred in the grip of ice, you know. The ten thousand year interglacial period is what humanity has enjoyed for a long time. In fact, we are now eight hundred years overdue for a new Ice Age."

"Eight hundred years overdue?"

"Oh yes. But naturally, the government think, 'Don't worry, sometimes the interglacial period lasts for up to twelve thousand years, so fingers crossed and let's hope we're out of office before the big freeze comes'. But now they are changing their minds, and it is perhaps too late. We have two years, if that."

"Is the panic justified, Professor? We've coped with terrible temperatures before, after all. In Medieval times, *the 'little ice age' in Britain brought such bad winters that fairs were held on the frozen Thames."*

"My dear, let me explain what happened at the height of the last Ice Age. Glaciers covered forty per cent of the world's surface, spreading out from the poles. There was land left, of course; but freezing night-time temperatures all year round, spring and summer, destroyed many sources of food. Crops died, and even if pre-civilized man had had the intelligence to farm them, it would have done very little good. Around the equator, in the tropics, rainfall dropped to almost nothing, and many of those regions warm enough to grow food became deserts through lack of moisture. During those hundreds of centuries, only small pockets of life could survive. The greater proportion of living things died, all across the Earth. The 'little ice age' was only a taste of what is to come."

"Is it really that bad?"

"The evidence is there. I have no doubt in my mind. Make no mistake, we stand on the brink of the worst catastrophe that mankind has ever encountered in recorded history."

"This is bullshit. This just *isn't* happening!" Wren said.

"It's happening, alright," Mayner replied.

They stood against a wall that ran high along a steep hillside. Beneath them, between the trees, was Endcliffe Park, lazing in the sun. An ice-cream van, its presence suddenly woefully ironic, stood on the pavement nearby as if desperate to sell its stock before it became obsolete. A small square of padded black rubber marked out the boundaries of a children's play area. Almost nobody was in sight. The Saturday traffic was a trickle. The city was in shock.

"Six hundred years ago, all the finest scientists in the world thought the Earth was flat. Nobody knew any different. Six hundred years is like . . . an eyeblink in history. They were wrong then, and they're wrong now."

"They're *not* wrong, Wren. Will you get over it?"

Wren looked at his friend in disbelief. "You're telling me to get *over* it? This isn't . . . it's not like my gran dying or something! This is the bloody *extinction* of our *species*!"

"So what, you're gonna spend the next two years or so worrying about it, making what's left of your life a misery?" Mayner said, dragging on a tab and looking quizzically at him. He shrugged. "That makes sense."

Wren's disbelief changed to bitter laughter. "God, Mayner, sometimes I envy the way you can only think five minutes ahead of yourself."

Mayner didn't reply for a time, just carried on looking out through the trees to the city beyond. When he did, it was to say: "Don't know why you're worried, anyway. We'll probably be ash by this time next week."

"I feel better already," Wren replied.

After hearing the announcement on Kayleigh's radio, they had rung Wren's dad from the mobile and gone home. Hardly anyone had said a word since the news. They just packed up their tents and left. It was a mutual understanding. The last thing they wanted to do right then was have fun.

It was the next morning when Wren called Mayner

and asked to meet him. Since then, they had talked about nothing but the war and the looming prospect of endless winter. The media called it 'The Big Freeze' after the comments of some Professor guy. The papers were full of nothing else, even ousting the endless trite articles on the affairs of the Royal Family for a time. One national tabloid started running cut-out-and-keep sections on coping with arctic climates, and the SAS Survival Handbook was sold out of shops and mail-order firms across the nation.

It was as if Wren had been given new eyes and ears, and he had not yet had time to adjust. Things around him had seemed to take on a clarity that was almost hyper-real. The shaking of the tree branches and the shadowplay they made on the dirt hillside they rested on seemed almost tearjerkingly beautiful. The words that they traded seemed, in contrast, utterly pointless. He noted every useless sentence, how roundabout and repetitive conversation was, as if he was an outsider watching two people in a discussion. Everything he saw or heard was now coloured with the sudden realization that it *might not be there for long*, and it forced him to assess his priorities ruthlessly.

He found himself thinking of Cass again. It seemed absurd that his mind should dwell on her, in the midst of everything, but it was out of his control. And suddenly, there by a wall above Endcliffe Park, he was struck by a sudden compulsion. At first it surprised him with its fury, but as it settled into him it seemed to make more and more sense, a morbid kind of logic.

"I'm gonna go and see her," he said.

"Kayleigh?"

"Cass."

"*Cass?*" Mayner exclaimed. "You nuts? You think she needs to deal with you on a day like this?"

"I've got to, Mayner. I dunno why. I've gotta do it now."

"You wanna clear stuff up with her?"

"I don't want. . ." Wren began, then trailed off. He adjusted his baseball cap to ease the chafe on his forehead. Mayner looked at him expectantly. "I don't want to . . . go to war or die or whatever, with her still mad at me. I wanna explain."

"You going now?" Mayner asked, rubbing the back of his neck where the sun had beat it red.

"I said I was, didn't I?"

Mayner made a low whistle. "Good luck, mate. I mean it."

"Thanks," Wren said, and left, trudging away down the too-bright streets.

Mayner didn't watch him go. Instead, he glanced up at the sky, where the blazing ball of the sun seared an after-image across his eyes. How could it have worked out this way? The last few decades had been the hottest ever. The planet was warming up, not heading for an endless winter.

He chuckled grimly to himself at the strange irony. Funny how you can prepare for anything, but the thing that comes along is always what you least expect. Who'd have thought? A bloody Ice Age. He had a sudden image of him and Jamie and Wren loping around in furs chucking spears at woolly mammoths, and burst out laughing.

*

Wren stood at the entrance to the drive for a long time.

Cass's house was a large, impressively well-kept structure, with an immaculate lawn and garden and a just-washed royal blue Jaguar basking in the sun outside the garage. The walls were a deep brown, the colour of mahogany, and bay windows bulged out of the lower two of its three storeys. Cass had the upper storey – a converted attic – all to herself. She was the only child of a rich family.

Wren felt himself on the verge of throwing up. His throat was tight and dry, and he could barely swallow. His stomach was making dull threats about ejecting its contents. His face felt hot and the skin taut.

What's the worst that can happen? They'll shout at you? It's nothing to get this wound up about.

But cold reason made not the slightest difference. He was more nervous than he had ever been in his life, and was dreading what he had to do. But that was the point. He *had* to do it.

Just start walking. Once you've started, there's no turning back.

He took a step, and drew it back before his sole touched tarmac. An old guy shuffled by, humiliating him simply by his presence, because he had seen Wren hanging around the front of Cass's house like a terrified burglar.

It was his disgust at himself that motivated him. Taking that first step was like stepping off a precipice, but he did it anyway, walking down the curving drive, his eyes fixed on the sanded-wood front door with its brass knocker and *kanji* pictograms etched down the frame. He ignored the knocker, resting his finger against the matching brass doorbell, and hesitated there for a second. Steeling himself, he took a breath and pressed it.

There were a few agonizing moments, and then he could hear someone walking towards the other side of the door. By her steps, he knew it was Cass. Her father had a much heavier tread and her mother . . . well, it wouldn't be her.

The door opened, and he was once again swamped by that awful, nameless emotion that had taken hold when he had seen her before. She was wearing the same baggy trousers, although her T-shirt had been switched for a plain leaf-green top and she was not wearing her beanie, her black hair falling free.

For a moment, neither of them said anything. In the end, it was she who spoke.

"*O-hisashiburi desu ne,*" she said coldly. It's a long time since we met.

He knew she wasn't counting Thursday's chance crossing of paths. "*Hai,*" he replied, his voice nearly failing him. It took him a moment to remember what little rudimentary Japanese he had picked up during their relationship. "*O-genki desu ka?*" Are you well? It was a pointless pleasantry, but his mind had fallen blank.

"*Genki desu,*" she replied, then stopped being intentionally awkward and switched to English. "I never thought to see you again."

"I never thought I'd be here."

Silence. She stood in the doorway, and she didn't invite him in. He hadn't expected her to.

"What do you want, Wren?" she asked, her tone making it clear that no quarter would be given.

"I . . . I wanted to talk with you," he said.

"Now? You didn't talk to me for more than a year and you want to talk now?"

"Cass, I know I didn't, but . . . well."

"*Well?*" she cried. "That's all you can say? What's brought on this sudden change of heart? Oh, wait, I can guess. You decided you want to shed some of your guilt before the war starts, am I right? Only four or five days left, is it?"

He winced. She had always been able to see into him with such effortless ease.

"It . . . provided the motivation," he said.

"You left me, Wren. You didn't even call. You didn't even *write*!" She was angry now. He knew the sight of him would have provoked a reaction like that. He deserved it, to be honest.

"I was afraid," he said, and the words weren't so hard to say as he had imagined.

"*Were* you?" she said, scathingly. "Well, I was *bereaved*, Wren, and having my boyfriend run out on me was hardly the best therapy, now was it?"

"Cass, I know, and I am *so* sorry."

She brushed her hair back from her face, her dark eyes blazing. "It's taken you all this time just to say that. Just to say sorry. You never once . . . even apologized."

"I . . . I couldn't face it. If I'd have said it aloud, I'd have . . . I dunno. I couldn't. Not to you."

"You never said sorry," she repeated, and suddenly her face tightened into tears. She launched herself at him, screeching: "You *bastard*! You *killed* my *mother* and you never even said *sorry*!"

Wren was too surprised to react, and she hit him hard across the face. A moment later, she was on him, a fury of anger, slapping and scratching and calling him every foul name she could think of. He tried to hold her off, but he couldn't restrain her without hurting her, so he tried to retreat from her; but she wouldn't let him go, pummelling him on her doorstep, and all he could do was shield his face and hope—

And then it stopped. She was still screaming and crying, but the blows ceased; and when he looked up, he saw her father there, a tall, thin Londoner with a thick mane of grey hair, holding her back. She gave up on her attempts at escaping his grip, and instead hugged him, sobbing into his chest. He never took his eyes from Wren's.

"I'm sorry," he said again, to both Cass and her father. The words came out numb.

"You'd better go," said the older man, but whether it was anger, disgust, weariness or kindness in his voice was impossible to tell.

Wren nodded, and walked back up the drive to the street, feeling his own self-loathing dragging him down to the ground, which waited to swallow him up.

Mayner stayed at the park for a good while after Wren left. Like everybody else, he had a lot to think about; and like everybody else, the real implications had not sunk in yet. The world was changing. Literally. And everyone was scrambling for the countries along the equator, because they knew that those countries would be the warmest and would escape the tide of mighty glaciers that would sweep out from the polar caps. Too little living space, too many people, and tensions were rising. War was on the horizon, getting closer with frightening speed. Unless someone hit on a solution fast, the human race wouldn't even survive to reach the Ice Age.

Wren was wrong about him. He *did* think more than five minutes into the future. It was just . . . it didn't *bother* him at all. He'd had too many times when he'd fretted about some event that had never come to pass. Despite what he'd said, he wouldn't be surprised if this one was just a false alarm as well. But he wasn't banking on it.

After a time, he left to make the walk home. If he was honest with himself, he'd rather have stayed on his own. The blank, listless, drifting forms of his parents – and, indeed, everyone else he had met except Wren – were hardly the best company. Since last night, everyone seemed to be wandering about in a zombie-like daze, not really listening to anything, wrapped up in their own concerns and a rapidly tattering shroud of disbelief. They were waking up one by one, but it took some longer than others. He didn't even dare think about talking to Jamie; the expression on his friend's face when he heard the Announcement (Mayner thought it merited a capital letter by now) was of such utter despair that he thought it best to stay away. He was never good at counselling people; he always just made them feel worse.

67

He took a long and winding route back, through the prettier districts between Hunters Bar and Nether Edge, where the houses were old and expensive and rested serenely in a nest of broad trees, their bricks cooking in the sun. He stayed in the dappled shade, feeling damp around the armpits and cursing the ineffectiveness of his anti-perspirant spray. His mind had drifted a considerable distance from his body when he ran into Tracksuit and Slacks.

It was just coincidence, that was all it was. There was no way they could have known he was here. And they had been the last people he had expected to see. Somehow, he always equated them with the more run-down, urbanized areas of Sheffield; they didn't belong in such attractive surroundings.

He saw them as he turned down a lane overhung with dangling leaves and flanked by newly-cut gardens. They were halfway up it, walking towards him, with three of their four subordinates in tow. Recognition flashed between them at the same moment, and then Mayner turned and ran.

It hadn't been his intention to flee. He should have just kept on walking, taken what was coming to him like a man. But he had no choice. Something inside him snapped. His courage had been tested first by the news of imminent war, then by the revelation of global disaster; this was too much. Barely healed from his last beating, he couldn't take another one; and Tracksuit's words were still fresh in his head from Thursday afternoon.

"Next time we meet, you puny shit, I'm gonna beat you

raw, and I'm not gonna stop till something breaks."

So he ran, and behind him he heard the sudden acceleration of footsteps as they gave chase.

His survival instincts shifted into gear immediately, his eyes scanning the area for possible escape routes. Sticking to the roads was suicide; they were older, taller and faster than him. The only way he'd beat them was by outmanoeuvring them.

No opportunity yet. Just run.

His constant smoking had left him unfit, even for someone who never exercised, and already he felt the unpleasant, sick-hot feeling of overexertion. Now that his pride had finally caved under the pressure of his fear, he was really *terrified*, dreading the possibility of yet another kicking. It lent him speed, and pushed him on, even though his lungs were beginning to sear, protesting at their sudden call to action.

He glanced behind him, saw them pounding after him. Gaining. Fast.

Goading himself to new speeds, he frantically cast about for a way to get off the wooded roads and into a place where he could avoid the pursuit. Still no real opportunity.

Screw it; take a chance.

He darted over the road and vaulted a low stone wall, landing in the front garden of one of the grand houses. This one was some kind of administration centre, open even on a Saturday, a huge, three-storey thing of grey stone with tall, thin windows behind which he could see pine desks, PCs and tidy secretaries working on them. A small car park flashed by to his right, but he was heading around the side of the building, following the grassy strip to where it widened into a pleasant patio lawn at the back.

A pair of suits were chatting on the concrete patio, whiskeys in hand. They turned to watch him indignantly as he tore across the grass, his soles thudding on the turf, and ran to the row of tall pines at the far end that screened the building from its neighbours. Pushing into them, he found another low wall on the far side, and clambered over it just as he heard the annoyed cry of somebody behind him, protesting at the five vandals who had pelted across the lawn in the wake of their prey.

Into another garden, this one a residential house that backed on to the office building. He fled through it, his ears beginning to whine with exertion and his cheeks burning, his centre-parted hair flopping against his face with a distracting lack of rhythm. The trees rustled and he looked back, and there was Tracksuit, forging through the pines, the anger plain on his face. He was even more irate now that he'd got his tracksuit scratched up.

Damn it, leave me alone! Mayner thought, and then realized that he had slowed down as his body flagged, and forced himself to pick up speed again.

Out of the garden, over a road, and he was in Nether Edge, where the streets were hotter and dustier, less greenery and more traffic. Kids were out playing on the streets, unaffected by the news of impending tragedy, and they looked up as he sprinted by. One of them even took the piss out of the way he ran. They shut up fast when Tracksuit and Slacks' gang arrived out of the garden, spilling on to the pavement and racing after their target.

Coming up to Abbeydale Road now, a main artery into the city, where there were always a lot of people and often police. He hated himself for thinking it, for chickening out and running to the cops, but right now he'd do anything to avoid being caught by the mob that pursued him. They had made up a good amount of distance on the downhill stretch through Nether Edge, and it would only be a matter of time. . .

The road was nearly empty. *Shit.* Only a few distant cars, one or two half-hearted shoppers drably exploring the few places that had bothered to open, and a sun-blasted stretch of tarmac with no help in sight. Seeing no other option, he bolted across the road and into the forecourt of an abandoned petrol station. Just behind there was an iron walkway over the railway tracks. Graffiti-strewn, rusted metal barriers blurred by on either side, his desperate footsteps changing from a thud to a clank as he crossed it; but it was only a moment before his pursuers' footsteps did the same, and he realized then that they were right behind him, maybe only an arm's length away, and nothing he could do would prevent what was about to happen.

He had just reached the end of the bridge when a foot snagged his leg, and he tripped, sprawling full-length on to the path on the far side. His hands blazed in pain as he stripped the skin off them in his attempt to save himself, his knee smashed into the ground, and then he was rolling uncontrollably, bruising himself in a dozen different places as he knocked himself against the tarmac.

He hadn't even come to a stop before the first kick reached him. As if this was the signal, the rest of them followed in a succession too fast to count. All sides, all over; his mind detached itself almost immediately as a reaction. He could feel the pain alright, but it was removed from him a little, for his brain could only calculate so much hurt at once and it was being overloaded by the barrage from all sides. Only particularly vicious ones snapped him back to attention; one that caught him across the jaw, one in his groin that made him vomit, a stamp on his head that smacked his skull against the tarmac of the path. But it was all buried, muted under a tide of misery and humiliation and rage and fear, so strong that it almost choked him, washed him away so that even the pain didn't seem worth caring about any more. *Let* them kill him. He wasn't bothered. Not now.

"*Oi!*"

The bellow cut through the miasma that surrounded him. It was rough and throaty, a tone that commanded respect because you just *knew* the person who owned it was nails. The kicking ceased with an immediacy that was unnatural, as if someone had pressed the PAUSE button on the whole affair. They stepped away from him slowly, backing off. For a long time, nobody spoke, but Mayner could almost sense the tension and fear in the air. With a great effort, he raised his head, levering open blackening eyes to see what the situation was.

It was the skinhead guy he had met outside the

school. The militant nationalist. He had a snarl like a dog on his face, and he was holding some huge-calibre handgun, a Desert Eagle or something, and had it levelled at Tracksuit.

"If I see any one o' you near my mate here again," he said, and there was something in his voice that said: *I'm not kidding here.* "I'm gonna put a hole in your chest the size of a dinner plate. We clear?"

Nobody replied. They were too terrified.

"Now *piss off*!" he roared, and they ran, scuttling away like startled dogs.

Mayner lay where he was, closing his eyes again, sunk in a mess of depression and pain the like of which he had never imagined. He heard the crunch of the skinhead's Docs as he walked over, replacing the gun in the underarm slide beneath his bomber jacket. There was a creak of denim as he squatted down.

"Come on, mate," he said, laying a hand on Mayner's shoulder. "Let's get you cleaned up."

CHAPTER SIX

"We're back with Professor Maliard, whom many of you will remember from yesterday's broadcast, for our special extended feature on what has become known as 'The Big Freeze'. Professor Maliard, I believe you coined that term on this very show less than twenty-four hours ago."

"You know, that's so typical of the tabloid media. They take a situation so grave that it questions the entire future of the human race and give it a catchy, cute little tag. Of course, why should they take it seriously? It's only the reason we've been brought to the brink of global conflict. It makes me wonder if any of what I have said has sunk in to their tiny little minds at all."

"Nevertheless, Professor, it was your words they were quoting."

"I'm not responsible if the media chooses to take my words out of context."

"Well, be that as it may, your appearance yesterday

generated a lot of feedback from the viewers. We have some letters for you later on, and you, the viewers, will be able to phone in on the number at the bottom of the screen and offer your opinions. But first, Professor. . . Could you please explain exactly how this disaster has occurred?"

"Certainly. You see, predicting the Ice Ages has been the work of scientists for a long time now. Many theories have come and gone. The work of a great man called Milankovitch was one of the first. Other scientists picked up his lead. Hamaker came up with a credible theory quite recently, about how the demineralization of the Earth's soil is causing our foliage to die slowly and rot, giving off CO_2, adding to the Greenhouse Effect that we ourselves are creating. This widens the world's climactic temperature differentials and evaporates the tropical oceans faster. This causes the polar glaciers to accumulate faster and travel towards the equator, hence the Ice Age begins."

"And that is what has happened here?"

"Partly. The real story is that the Atlantic Conveyor is about to switch off."

"The Atlantic Conveyor?"

"It is a current that brings tropical water to the North Atlantic across the sea. It's a huge thing, equivalent to seventy or eighty Amazon rivers. And it provides thirty per cent of Europe's atmospheric heat. It was brought to light by a scientist known as Wallace Broecker, quite recently in fact. When it cuts off, temperatures will plunge very suddenly and very sharply."

"But why is it about to switch off?"

"It is a little difficult to explain. It is called a conveyor because it works like a conveyor belt; one warm layer on top running towards the North Atlantic and a cool layer beneath, running away from it, back to the tropics. When salt water is cooled by the arctic winds, it becomes denser and sinks, creating convection – which is the mechanism that drives the conveyor. But if fresh water floods the surface of the sea above the conveyor, the salt water is diluted and is not dense enough to sink. The chain breaks down, and the conveyor stops."

"But why should fresh water—"

"My dear lady, the Greenhouse Effect, of course. The polar ice caps are melting, they have been for many years now. Icebergs break off and travel south and melt in the North Atlantic, dumping fresh water all over the Atlantic Conveyor. The same thing triggered the last Ice Age. Natural carbon dioxide accumulation from dying plants. Now it is happening again, and there is little or nothing we can do to stop it."

"It's amazing to think that such a trigger has been lying there for so long."

"The Earth is a complex system, and it is more fragile than we like to believe. If only one tiny part of the balance is upset, the whole thing falls apart. Mankind has been doing its best to kill itself since the Industrial Revolution, but it seems Mother Earth has finally tired of the damage we are doing, and decided to do the job herself."

Cassandra Tiller considered herself something of a messed-up girl.

It hadn't always been like that. She'd been confident, sure of herself, happy in the knowledge that she could handle any emotional situation. She could predict her own reaction and cope with it. Confronting dishonest friends, facing up to bitchiness, dealing with keeping and losing boyfriends; no problem. Except with Wren. The only one who had ever been able to throw her.

She'd gone out with him because he made her laugh. Nothing serious, more because she had something of a competition going with her friend at the time to see who could land the most boys by flirting outrageously with them. Childish, but then she was only young at the time. But when she really *fell* for him . . . well, she hadn't expected that at all. Too rapid. Her mother had told her not to get too involved, it was very easy to *think* you were in love at her age, but she knew even then that it was more than that. They were just . . . compatible. As good a match as anyone could hope for. They played off each other perfectly, each one bringing out and highlighting the best points in the other. It was love, she thought.

She still hadn't decided whether her mother was right or not.

Then, *that* day. How excruciatingly pathetic that someone's entire life, everything they had worked for and hoped for and dreamed about, can be smashed to pieces in the space of a single minute. It made her depressed to think about it. Life, love, money, society; all of them like a thin sheet of sugar glass over an abyss. People spend years building on it and then feel surprised and betrayed when it cracks beneath them.

Eighteen months now, since her mother died. Seventeen or so since Wren ran off and never spoke to her again. They only lived three miles apart, but she had never once come across him until that time outside the record store, where she'd gone looking for the new Alkaline Trio album and found herself leaving with a Feeder EP which she hated.

Still, eighteen months. And she still found herself weeping uncontrollably in the middle of the street, or getting panic attacks while sitting at home in the lounge, or becoming almost suicidally depressed in the middle of a movie for no reason. She still didn't trust herself. Her emotions, which had once been stable and easily navigable ground, had become a treacherous marsh, where every step could be a sinkhole or a quagmire. Eighteen months, and she still hadn't got over it.

And now Wren had turned up on her doorstep. To make peace, she guessed. To say sorry. After all this time.

And she found herself bloody well forgiving him.

It was ridiculous. She was actually fighting *against* the feeling, doing her best to come up with reasons why it *was* his fault, how he'd acted cruelly towards her, how he was spineless and a coward for deserting her. But it was like trying to hold back a tidal wave with a saucepan lid. Just to have heard him apologize . . . was that all that was propping up her precious anger? And now he'd done that, now he'd said he was sorry and *meant* it (she knew him well enough to tell), now all the anger and hate felt fake. Like she was just pretending to be mad because she thought she should be.

She was forgiving him, and she couldn't stop herself.

It was raining hard as she walked home from church. She was not particularly religious – she'd never really given the matter much thought, truth be told, even after her mother's funeral – but she'd felt the need today for even the smallest reassurance. Most of Sheffield had felt the same way, judging by the packed pews. There was barely standing-room left by the time she had arrived. Prayers were said, asking for God's intervention to save them from catastrophe. She joined in with the words, but ended up leaving halfway through. What was the point of prayer if you couldn't concentrate enough to mean it? She was thinking of Wren.

The sun had been swallowed by a freak gathering of rainclouds during the twenty minutes she had spent inside, and as she left they opened up on her in disapproval. She was glad of them. The heat had taken on a faintly sinister quality, its very presence reminding everyone that it would not be there for much longer. In contrast, the rain on her skin felt honest, at least. Water triumphs over fire, as it always does eventually.

She walked down the slick, paved plaza towards the subway underpass that led to her home. Her eyes were on the ground in front of her, thinking of things other than where she was going, her sodden hair braided into a long queue behind her, her trainers raising little splash-footprints as she passed that were gone in less than a second.

"Invasion started already?" said a voice ahead of her. She looked up, and there, sheltering in the subway, was a short, stocky man with a severe grey crew-cut. He was wearing tight jeans, army boots, and wearing the ubiquitous black bomber jacket of his organization. She knew who he was, alright. One of those UKCDF psychos.

"What?" she asked, pouring the appropriate amount of scorn and defiance in her voice.

"I *said*, has the invasion started already? Didn't know you Chinks had made it over here yet."

She stopped at the entrance to the subway. He was halfway down it, lounging against the brick of the tunnel.

"I'm Japanese, not Chinese, you moron," she said.

"S'no difference, is there?" he said, shrugging and giving her an infuriatingly cheeky smile. "You're all slants, ain'tcha?

"If you say so," she replied, giving him a scathing look.

They stood there for a moment, looking at each other, she in the rain and he in the shelter of the subway.

"Well?" she said.

"Well what?"

"You gonna let me past?" she asked, angrily.

"Am I stopping you?" he replied, question for question.

She considered the options. Part of her wanted to walk right past the xenophobic lump of filth just to show that she wasn't afraid. The other part, that *was* afraid, was stronger, and backed up by common sense. She didn't want to go near him. He could be dangerous. The point of pride wasn't worth the risk.

With a dismissive tut, she turned away and

disappeared from the subway entrance, taking the path up a grassy bank to where the dual carriageway was. She'd rather chance the traffic.

She felt almost violated on the rest of the way home, sick with anger, frustrated that one man's bigoted ignorance should have such an effect on her. But it wasn't just him. He was just the start of it.

People were getting scared. They needed targets. And by virtue of her mother's blood, she was lucky enough to be one.

Jamie lay on his bed and stared at the ceiling. His Minidisc paused as it shuffled around the tracks on one of his compilation albums, then finally settled on something drum 'n' bassy that he had forgotten the name of. It was dark outside. He could feel the darkness, even though his curtains were shut. Rain hissed and rattled beyond the pane, as it had been doing for a long while now. The bulb that hung from the centre of the ceiling was muted by the colourful paper-star shade that surrounded it, flooding the room in soft yellow-red light.

There were no answers. There was no way out.

He had not moved for most of the afternoon and evening, except to change the disc every so often, and once to get a sandwich from the kitchen. It frightened him. Never before had he *thought* so much. The minutes had slid by, leaving no memory of their presence, and before he knew it he had been there for five or six hours. Thinking. And with every dead end, every stillborn option, his panic increased, until it clouded his mind and stopped him thinking straight.

Option a) he would be killed in a nuclear strike. Sheffield was one of the primary targets in England in the event of an attack. Its industries were essential for any war effort. The Eastern Alliance would just *love* to see Sheffield as a smoking heap of slag.

Option b) no nukes, just war. In which case he would be conscripted, sent to fight in some malaria-ridden jungle, and die with his legs shredded by a landmine. He'd seen enough films and documentaries about Vietnam to know what it would be like.

Option c) there wouldn't be a war. Unlikely. And then they'd have the Big Freeze to deal with, which was even worse.

That was it, as far as he could tell. That was what his hours of hard thinking had distilled from the whirl of fears in his head.

He was trapped. There was absolutely no way to turn. Whichever way he looked, whichever possibility he considered, it meant the same thing. Everything he had known in his life up to this point was going to be torn apart. Every rock that he had clung to, every star he had navigated by, it would all be gone. He was facing an utter rearrangement of his world, either by the power of a faceless government official or by some omnipotent natural force.

Like a kid caught in a maze, his parents lost, his terror growing with every wrong turn as he realizes he might never get out. And the seconds were ticking away, drawing them inexorably closer to disaster. Four days, that was all. Four short days till the deadline expired.

The tune on his Minidisc had just cut down to a drum-only breakbeat when the tears came.

It only made things worse. Every time he had cried in the past – and he was not a cryer by nature; it took a lot to bring him to that point – he had always felt better afterwards. Something about the release of tears seemed to let off the pressure, made it all not so bad. This time, long after his tears had been wiped away on a corner of his blanket, the suffocating sensation remained. The tightness in his chest, his throat, the pounding in his head.

There

was

no

escape.

He got up suddenly, throwing himself to his feet as if in disgust, and stamped out into the corridor to the bathroom next door. He took off his glasses, locked the door behind him, ran the hot tap until it was scalding, and then splashed his face with it, ignoring the burn on his palms and fingers. He rubbed it into his eyes, massaging his face hard, and looked in the mirror. His face looked surprisingly normal to him, considering the abject fear that lay behind it. Reddened and wet from the water, there was no evidence of his tears except his bloodshot eyes. He could have just been tired.

Towelling off his face, he went downstairs into the lounge. His body felt fragile, as if it might just unravel as he walked, as if he might break down again. But he had to . . . he had to tell *someone*. He needed help, needed support. Not from his friends, no. He couldn't face their sympathy. But from *him*, instead. The one man whose support he had never been able to get.

The lounge was arranged so that the chairs faced away from the door he entered through, angled towards the TV on the far wall. Soft lighting from flower-shaped smoked glass receptacles spread across the brown and beige décor. A warm room, cosy and homely. Where his mother was, he didn't know. She was rarely at the house, preferring to spend her time at one of her various social clubs. But his father was there, his ruthlessly trimmed nape and tight ginger crew-cut visible above the back of one of the easy chairs.

He stopped in the doorway. His father would have heard the door open, as the handle rattled loudly whenever it was twisted and the door squeaked against the jamb. His father knew he was there, alright. It was just that he gave no indication of caring.

Jamie felt tears suddenly start to his eyes again. If that didn't sum up their relationship perfectly. Such a neat thought; Wren would have been proud of him.

It was just that his father never was.

He stepped back into the kitchen, closing the door behind him and somehow managing to make it silent. For a long moment, he paused there. Then, wearing only a thin shirt, jeans and socks, he walked out of the front door into the slashing onslaught of the rain and was swallowed by the darkness.

CHAPTER SEVEN

"Welcome back. If you joined us during the break, this edition is devoted to one subject only: nuclear war. Exploring the truths, exposing the myths, talking to the experts to let you know what is really likely to happen if the worst should occur. With only three more days to go before the NATO deadline is reached, and with the Eastern Alliance showing no sign of slowing their advance, prospects are looking grim. Vietnam and Laos have fallen to the Chinese and Mongolians, with Thailand and Cambodia now under threat. The Philippines, Malaysia, Indonesia and Papua New Guinea are under the control of Russian Federation forces. Somalia is under attack by Kazakhstan. This programme is in no way suggesting that nuclear war is a likelihood, but I think we all have to accept that it is an immediate possibility. And we must be prepared for it.

"The following information may alarm you, but I urge

you to stay tuned, because it may one day be necessary to know these things. This is John Keller, a NATO nuclear scientist, and he will be explaining exactly what occurs during a nuclear strike."

"Thank you. Yeah, the details are really not pretty, but it is necessary to know them. For the purposes of this explanation, I'll be using a model of a five megaton bomb exploded at ground level. That's the equivalent of five million tons of TNT. That's not especially large by today's standards, but to give you some idea of how big that is, let me say that the bomb that destroyed Hiroshima was only 12.5 kilotons, or 12,500 tons of TNT.

"First there would be the flash. The flash of an exploding nuclear device is intense enough to melt your eyeballs if you are looking directly at it. Others would be blinded by the sight. Some may recover, most won't; and for a large proportion, it would be too late by then. The fireball at Ground Zero is nearly as hot as the centre of the Sun. Everything within a couple of miles of the epicentre is annihilated, blasted and scorched in a howling, shrieking inferno before being sucked upwards into the clouds where it will return to the ground later as radioactive fall-out. A heat wave blasts out from the centre, setting fire to just about everything that can burn, and that's closely followed by a shockwave strong enough to pulverize a skyscraper. You can expect winds of up to 330 miles per hour in its wake.

"Up to about three and a half miles from Ground Zero, you can expect pretty much total destruction. Nothing survives. The power of the blast diminishes with distance, but you can expect most buildings to be

burning or knocked into rubble all the way up to about a ten mile radius from the centre. Injuries, seventy-mile-an-hour winds all the way out to eighteen and a half miles from the blast. People who aren't killed by the shockwave or the heat get crushed under rubble as their houses collapse on them, or thrown about by the winds. And then, finally, it all calms. The survivors begin to pick themselves up. And that's when the fall-out starts coming down.

"See, by now there's an enormous black cloud of dust over everything, which is what is left of everything that was at the centre of the explosion. It comes drifting down in little flakes of ash. But what you can't see is that the ash is loaded with lethal radiation. If that stuff touches you, you're dead. First you feel tired, and you just want to sleep all the time, but you're throwing up constantly. You get diarrhoea, your gums bleed, your hair comes out in clumps. And you're in agony. Then, after a few days, suddenly you get better. You think it's all over. But it's only half-time. The radiation is in your bone marrow by now. You've shaken off the first lot, but it's coming back. A few weeks later you get sick again, and this time there's no recovery. You die."

Wren was remembering happier days, watching something on the TV without really registering it. The burn of talking to Cass after all this time had still not faded, and he still loathed himself. How could he have let it go on so long? How could he have left it a *year and a half*? How utterly gutless was that? He had ruined their relationship by an accident, but he had alienated her by his own cowardice, because he couldn't face up to what he had done.

And the memories he'd thought he had buried had come swarming back as he lay wallowing in misery. The days they'd snuggled together on her bed – her room, because she had a TV – watching martial arts movies and Twin Peaks reruns; the time he'd gone on holiday with her and her folks to Nagoya, visiting her mother's family; the first time they'd slept together. . .

But with the good memories came the bad ones. And, as he sat watching whatever passed for entertainment at eleven o'clock on a Monday morning when he should have been at school, he found himself unable to stop the pictures playing across his head, clear and sharp and dreadful.

A cold midwinter day, frost edging the panes of the Tillers' kitchen. It was that kind of temperature where it was possible to feel the edge of the conflict, the point where the heat and the chill met and battled, so that it sometimes seemed cool and crisp even though the room was baking. There was a sparkling new Aga against one wall, dark green, the handles of its doors made of shiny black metal. Cass's mother was cooking on it, juggling pots full of boiling vegetables and trays of roast potatoes.

Her name was Michiko, and by the time she died she had practically adopted Wren as a son. He could never sit around and talk with his own parents, and certainly not Mayner's or Jamie's, but Michiko Tiller was one of the kindest and most genuinely warm-hearted people he had ever met. Her childhood in rural Japan was a fascinating source of conversation, just for the sheer difference in culture to the British way of life. She always seemed happy to see Wren, always liked to hear what he had been doing and how his life was. And more, she accepted him, without any of the wariness that some parents – Cass's father, for one – might show towards the boyfriend of their daughter.

She was a plump woman, who habitually wore fisherman's jumpers with long dresses while around the house. Her black hair was gathered in a tight bun behind her head. It was how Wren always remembered her, how she had been on that day.

Cass had gone out on a driving lesson, leaving Wren to amuse himself for an hour. It was nothing new; she was often having to run off on errands or suchlike, and he was comfortable enough in the house to hang around without feeling awkward. So he sat chatting with Michiko. He couldn't really recall what it was they were talking about, only the moment when she suddenly turned away from the stove with a strange, taut expression on her face.

"Andrew. . ." she said thinly, calling him by his first name as was her habit, and then sank slowly to the kitchen floor, clutching her jumper in her fist between her breasts.

Wren didn't react for a moment; he was too alarmed and bewildered. Then it passed, and he jumped out of his chair, banging his knees against the kitchen table, and scrambled over to crouch by her. She was lying on the floor, her jumper still gathered in her fist, her eyes staring and breathing rapid and shallow.

"Andrew . . . pills. . ." she said, her voice distressingly hoarse. "My pills . . . get them. . ."

"Where are they?" he asked automatically. Pills? What pills? How long had he known her, and neither she or Cass had ever mentioned—

"Bathroom. . ." she said. "By the sink. . ."

The medicine cabinet. Dumb. He should have known. He got up and ran into the bathroom. Where was Cass's father? It was a Saturday, he wasn't at work. Where *was* he?

Into the bathroom, and he tore open the mirrored cabinet above the sink and looked inside. All kinds of pharmaceuticals, so familiar to him that he didn't notice them any more whenever he reached inside for his toothbrush: toothpaste, Strepsils, a tube of Anusol that always made him laugh when he thought about it, and a bunch of small white pill bottles from the chemists. He had never really thought about their purpose, reasoning that it was none of his business; now he wished he had looked more closely at them. A half-full bottle of penicillin; co-proxamol from when Cass's father had broken his arm; and another one with an indecipherable medical name which he didn't recognize. That had to be it.

He grabbed the pills, running back into the kitchen. Michiko was clawing at the air with one hand, the other one still wrapped in her jumper. Her eyes were sheened with frenzy, and though they turned to him as he entered, she didn't seem to register him. He knelt down next to her, his heart thumping in fright, and scanned the label on the bottle.

Take two with water as necessary.

It's bloody necessary now, he thought, unscrewing the childproof cap. He wished that the label had something printed on it other than the name and instructions for use, like what the hell he was dealing with, what was happening to his girlfriend's mother right now. But no, it was frustratingly vague, so he grabbed a glass from the draining-board, half-filled it with water, shook two of the dry white pills into his hand and put them in Michiko's mouth. She seemed to fasten on to the fact that he was trying to help her, that the pills were what she needed, and she became suddenly lucid, taking them into her mouth and accepting the swallow of water he gave her. She relaxed almost immediately, settling back to the floor with a sigh.

He put the pills aside, then ran into the lounge to grab a cushion and slipped it under her head. She had closed her eyes as if in relief, her breathing slowing and steadying. He ran back into the lounge, picked up the phone and rang the number he had never hoped to need, nine-nine-nine, and it was a rotary phone so it took ages for the three numbers to connect. He called an ambulance. He went back to the kitchen.

Which was when he saw that Michiko had stopped breathing altogether.

It was the second-worst feeling he had ever experienced, and he would rather have died himself than have to go through it again. The realization of what was happening sledgehammered into him, and he lost it. He didn't remember the next ten minutes. He had a vague recollection of trying to do CPR on her, but he didn't know what he was doing and it didn't work. He could still taste the frustration and terror as he knew he could do nothing to prevent her slipping away.

The next thing he remembered was the sirens and the doorbell, and letting in the paramedics. They tried their best, but no good. He went with her to hospital. She was dead on arrival.

Some kind of heart condition, they said. She'd been on medication. Nothing he could have done. Probably he would have been too late anyway. Except that he had not fed her the pills the doctor had prescribed her in case of an attack, he had fed her the migraine suppressants that she had been given a year ago or so to help her over her infrequent attacks. The real drugs she needed were by the sink, like she said. In full view, standing in the little dip in the ceramic where the soap was usually kept. He hadn't seen them.

The pills didn't kill her; they were harmless in small doses. They just weren't the drugs she needed. So his being *probably* too late wasn't good enough. *Probably* wasn't *definitely*. He *could* have saved her.

But he hadn't. He'd killed her instead.

The hospital called Cass at her home, and she came right over. It was the longest, most agonizing fifteen minutes he had experienced up until that point, waiting for her to arrive, knowing that . . . knowing that he had to tell her what he'd done, what had happened. He remembered every clumsy word he said, every tear-choked syllable, his voice flattened and dulled by a sorrow and self-loathing that gripped his throat from inside. And that was the worst thing he had ever felt in his life, worse even than watching Michiko die; the look on Cass's face, that moment when she finally understood the whole picture, that second when she teetered on the verge of a howling chasm of grief and looked pleadingly at him, as if he could save her, tell her it was all a joke.

But it was him who had put her there, and she had nowhere else to turn.

He stood with her as she gripped the edge of her mother's hospital bed, her shoulders juddering as she wept. He did not dare touch her, to put a comforting arm around her shoulders. How could the murderer comfort the daughter of his victim? The hospital staff had left them alone while they tried to contact Cass's father.

"How could you not see them?" Cass whispered. She hadn't spoken for so long that Wren was too taken aback to register what she actually said.

"What?" he said automatically.

"I said *how could you not see them*?" she shrieked, rounding on him suddenly, her face blotched and twisted in fury. "The pills, the bloody *pills*! They were on the damn sink, you *idiot*! All you had to do was get them for her! It wasn't too hard, was it? *Was it?*"

"I . . . Cass, I didn't know," he stammered, taking a step back. "I didn't know what was wrong with her, I didn't know what pills to—"

He was interrupted by a slap across his face, hard enough to rock his head to the side. "You *stupid bastard*!" she howled. "You . . . she's my. . ." The anger suddenly seemed to snuff out, leaving only an achingly fragile little girl. "She's dead, Wren. She's dead."

Wren couldn't reply. He could feel an unpleasant moistness on the side of his neck, and he put his hand to it. His fingertips came away smeared with a thin film of greasy blood. Just under the line of his jaw, a long scratch was oozing red. It was all but invisible in everyday life; but the scar from the ring Cass wore never healed.

Cass looked at his hands and then at his face. "Get out," she said. "I don't want you here."

It got worse after that. The next four weeks were a nightmare. The police involvement was mercifully brief, but that was the least of his worries. Cass was alternately hostile and sullen with him, although once or twice she cried on his shoulder. He expected it. He deserved worse than she gave him. And through it all, she never turned him away for more than a day at a time. Sometimes she hit him as she raged and wept; sometimes she hugged him as if he, the cause of her pain, was the only thing that could salve it.

But it wasn't Cass that drove him away. What was unbearable was how he felt about himself. He couldn't stand the constant guilt, the endless reminder that she represented. It sickened him inside, like a tree rotting at its heart, and every time he was with her the decay accelerated. He began to hate himself, really *hate* himself. And it swamped and suffocated him, closing in all around, until there was only one way out. He left her.

For a time, he was a mess. It was the knowledge that he couldn't face his girlfriend, that he was willing to take the shame of leaving her rather than see the hurt in her eyes one more time. That he was a coward. It tore and worried at him, tattering him. But while it was almost too much to take at first, it soon began to fade. Without Cass there to remind him, he could gradually, subtly push it aside, until bit by bit he learned to live with himself once more. He ran from her, and he never went back, shoving the skeleton in his closet where it grew and grew until the wood creaked under the weight of the accumulated bones.

Well, he thought, as the TV programme that he wasn't watching slewed into advert, *not any more. Time to have a clearout.*

The doorbell rang, like a buzzer on a gameshow indicating that his answer had won him a bonus square.

He got up to answer it, a little annoyed that he should be interrupted just on the point of a revelation. It was Kayleigh. Obviously she wasn't going to school either. He wondered if anyone would. The threat of detention seemed pretty weak at this point.

"Hi," she said, beaming sunnily.

"Hey, Kayleigh," he replied. The strange lack of enthusiasm at seeing her surprised him as much as it did her, for some of it bled into his voice. He was lucky that she shrugged it off.

"Don't sound happy to see me or anything," she grinned.

"Sorry. Just got up a minute ago," he lied. "Come in."

"Where's your parents?" she asked as she stepped into his house, then gave him a swift kiss before he could answer.

"Mmm. Girlfriend for breakfast," he said as they parted. She laughed, apparently in a particularly high mood. "Mam and Dad are away visiting friends. This whole Ice Age thing has got everybody that the NATO deadline didn't. The world's going slowly nuts, and everyone's started counting the seconds. So what's got you so spry today?"

"You not heard?" she asked, waltzing past him and beginning to make some coffee. "Hallam FM have been talking about it all morning. There's a peace rally in the city centre the day after tomorrow. A protest against war, to get the governments to stop squabbling and work out how to cope with the Big Freeze."

"Oh right," Wren said, which was wiser than saying what he thought: *lot of good that'll do.* But he knew it appealed to Kayleigh's pacifist streak, so he kept his opinions to himself.

"They reckon there's gonna be a few thousand there at least. They're calling it Stop the Countdown."

"Snappy," Wren replied.

She looked round from where she was pouring from the Pyrex jug that sat on the hotplate of the coffee machine. "You *are* in a bear of a mood today, aren't you?"

"Sorry, Kayleigh. It's just I've got a lot on my mind, what with the whole imminent death thing and all."

"What's your *problem*? You know, you've got to—"

"I went and saw Cass yesterday," he said, turning his back and leaning on the dining table with his knuckles.

"Oh," she replied, heaping several tonnes of meaning into a single syllable.

"Yeah, *oh*," he said.

"What did she say?" came the question, kept carefully level so as not to betray any emotion, and betraying it anyway.

"Not a lot. She attacked me."

"You surprised?"

"Not really," he said.

Kayleigh stirred the coffees and put one down in front of Wren. He didn't turn around. She went over to the latticed window and looked out over the garden.

"Why did you go and see her?"

"Because I wanted to make it up with her," he said. He had been intending to skirt round the issue, but in that moment he had decided that the deception was too pathetic to bother with.

"God, Wren, why do you want to put yourself through all that crap?" she said, and her voice was getting steadily sharper, honing itself on the whetstone of his words. "Isn't it enough that it happened? I've told you a million times it wasn't your fault, and it's never made any difference. What brought this on? You really think you're gonna die? You want to make everything okay before the final credits roll?"

"That's about the size of it," he said. He could tell by her tone that she wouldn't understand, even if he explained it all.

"You think you can just wipe away the last year just like that?"

"It was eighteen months," Wren said.

"I'm talking about *us*! You and me!"

Wren turned slowly around in his chair to face her,

both puzzled by her comment and annoyed at the implication. She was flushed and angry, her coffee forgotten.

"Kayleigh, I'm not getting back together with her or anything," he said.

"I never said that. But you were apparently thinking it."

"Me?" Wren said, his voice rising in volume. "Could you *be* more obviously jealous? When have I ever given you any reason to think I'd go back to Cass?"

"Don't you think I *know*?" Kayleigh shrieked. "That I can't tell, when you talk about her, that she was so much *better* and more *wonderful* than I am? You never say it, but it's there. Did you ever really break up with her, Wren? I mean, in your head, has she ever stopped being your girlfriend? Shit, you know how *long* I've lived in her shadow?"

Wren put his hands to the sides of his head in frustration. "Of course I talk about her; she was the biggest part of my life until recently. What do you want me to do, forget it all?"

"It's not that you talk about her, it's *how* you talk about her."

"And how *do* I talk about her?" Wren said, giving her a patronizing please-explain-you-petty-little-girl look.

"If you don't know, it's not worth telling you," she replied, flicking her blonde hair up in a movement that was supposed to be dismissive but came across as ridiculous.

"Meaning you don't know what you're talking about," said Wren, relishing the sudden blaze in her eyes at the insult. "Meaning you're just trying to vent whatever stupid jealous crap you've got built up inside you in any way you can. Go away if you're gonna do that, Kayleigh. I've got better things to be getting on with."

"What, like going and seeing Cass? Let her beat you up some more?" she shrieked.

"As opposed to being bitched at by you? I know which I'd choose right now." Deliberately pitched to hurt, and his aim was good. He returned his gaze to the table, not looking at her any more, knowing he'd scored the final point. True to his prediction, she walked out without a word. He could feel her anger, and he heard it as she slammed the front door, but he didn't have to see it, at least.

Failing another girlfriend, he thought. *At least I'm consistent.*

CHAPTER EIGHT

"But Doctor, how can you predict with any degree of accuracy how people will respond to something like this?"

"I would remind other members of the panel that there is a long history of precedent. Many times in the past, humankind has been convinced that the world will end, or that disaster is imminent. Incas, tribes all across the world . . . just because they did not have science to back them up did not make their belief any less strong. Why, speaking of science, only a short while ago we were told – by scientists – that a meteor big enough to wipe out life on Earth was heading towards us. It was at least a couple of days before it was established that it would miss us, but in that time, did civilization fall apart? I think not."

"You're being flippant. The fact is that humans are basically driven by instinct, just as animals are. This is especially true when humans are considered as a mass and not as individuals. When faced with impending disaster, they will become scared, panicky, and most likely irrational. Look at the situation in America; riots are already beginning in the inner cities of most of the major metropoli. The Big Freeze and the NATO deadline have turned these cities into tinderboxes, and it only takes the slightest spark to set them burning."

"We're talking Britain here, not America. I think you underestimate the size of the difference between our cultures, beneath the veneer of MTV and movies and so on.

"You're talking about the mythical 'British reserve', that is obviously a big factor in our appalling record for football hooliganism and violence abroad."

"The only thing more likely to cause violence than war is sport."

"Very droll. You're ducking the issue, however."

"No, this is the issue. Should we expect an outbreak of violence in Britain as in America? No. We didn't in World War Two, or World War One. Or the Cuban Missile Crisis, which bears a striking resemblance to this NATO deadline. In times of uncertainty, people just carry on with what they are doing. Routine is an important part of modern life. Shops may close temporarily, but they'll soon be open again. When a person cannot directly do anything about his or her situation, he or she will just get on with their normal day. Humans have a remarkable capacity to block out reality when they can't physically see or touch it."

"You're forgetting one thing. This is not just about the

NATO deadline. Even if we should get past that, there is something infinitely larger and darker waiting behind it, and nobody has any idea how we will cope with that. How will a person react if he believes he has no future? What will happen to responsibility then? Who fears the law in the face of death?"

Tuesday morning was dank and gloomy, sullenly holding on to the memory of the recent rains. Dark-bellied clouds hove low across the Sheffield hills, doing slow fly-bys, threatening to drop their load and never delivering. The air was tinny and thin, even when Mayner dragged on his tab. Everything tasted like shit today.

He walked with his shoulders hunched up and a slight scowl on his face. He was wearing a thigh-length Billabong snowboard jacket to combat the sudden cold weather. It didn't really matter; he couldn't much feel the cold anyway, unless he thought about it.

But whatever clothes he had been wearing since Saturday afternoon, that scowl had never left his face. It had etched itself into his features, without him even realizing it. An outward indication of what was going on inside him.

He had been angry and depressed in equal measure since the beating he had suffered at the hands of Tracksuit and Slacks and their mob. Mad with rage that they had made him crack and run, ashamed that his own pride had failed him and he had fled.

He could remember the exact moment when the trigger inside him tripped, when the years he had suffered at the hands of an endless stream of bullies had finally caught up with him. When he couldn't shrug and laugh it off any more. That moment when he had seen Tracksuit and Co at the other end of the picturesque, wooded street and his nerve had snapped.

He knew they were scared by the impending threat that hung over them all. He knew their only way to express their fear was through violence. It didn't matter.

It came down to this: either he spent the rest of his life being kicked, humiliated and abused, or he stopped it now. And what did he have to lose? Two days left, that was all. They'd probably all be dead by Thursday, and if not by then, then certainly by two years from now. The world was about to hit chaos, and nobody would care about whatever a seventeen-year-old boy from Sheffield did while they were trying to organize an effective defence against disaster.

Just as nobody would care if a few going-nowhere street thugs like Tracksuit and Slacks dropped off the planet. Oh, sure, a few clothes shops might mourn, a few underdressed tarts might miss out on disappointing sexual experiences, a few E-dealers might go home with fifteen quid less in their pocket than they would have otherwise; but nobody who counted would give a toss.

God, he could almost taste the bitterness on the back of his teeth.

It made him feel surprisingly good. He didn't realize how much everything had been getting on top of him. He'd even been fooling himself, persuading himself that he didn't care about the bag of crap his life had been ever since secondary school. Every time he seemed to be getting up, making a little bit of happiness for himself, he was brought right back to the bottom by some kid looking for an easy target. In the end, he'd stopped trying. Yeah, he was a mouthy little wide-boy. He also cried himself to sleep some nights, when he was sure nobody would hear him.

Was it the deadline? Probably. Wren had the right idea. It wasn't just a deadline for the Eastern Alliance. It was a deadline for everyone. Get your affairs in order. Sort everything out. *Be watchful, therefore, for ye know not when the master of the house doth come.* Guess he *had* been paying attention in Religious Ed classes, at least on one occasion.

Kayleigh had been in a state when he went to see her earlier today. He supposed all this stuff with her father was getting on top of her. She hadn't even noticed the freshly fading bruises on his face. It made him feel vaguely bad that he'd been so preoccupied with his own, secret reason for going round to her house that he'd not been too interested in what she was saying. As to the others, he hadn't talked to Wren or Jamie since he'd been beaten; they still didn't know. Good. This was his problem.

He reached the house, a terraced property in a dank and dismal street, and went round the back alley as he had been told. Planks of wet, rotted wood clattered under his feet. He found a flaking green fire-door and knocked on it. After a moment, it was opened.

It was the skinhead from UKCDF. He was still wearing the black bomber jacket and jeans.

"Hey, Jester," Mayner said.

"Alright, mate."

Mayner stepped inside, and Jester closed the door behind him.

Today was the day. He was going to see Cass, and he was going to even things out. Somehow. He didn't expect her to forgive him; in fact he expected her to spit at him. But he also knew that if she did, he would come back again and again until some kind of conclusion was reached. The first time had been the hardest. But seeing her, even though she was blind with hatred for him, had reminded him of what he had forgotten. Once, he had cared more about making this girl happy than anything. Maybe that was why he had been unable to face her grief, knowing that he had caused it. But now he *had* faced it, at least in some small measure. And the only thing worse than seeing her hate for him was knowing that she was not happy.

If letting her vent her anger on him was what she needed, then that was what he deserved. The *least* he deserved.

It had taken him hours of doing stupid, meaningless tasks around the house before he had finally run out of patience with himself. He had deliberated with himself whether he should really go, and how Kayleigh would react. It was the worst possible thing to do as far as their relationship was concerned. But this was *Cass*.

He had been walking to the front door when the phone rang, as if to make a last-minute save, delay a few more moments. He thought about not answering it, but then thought that – crazy idea – it might be Cass. So he picked up.

"Hello?"

"Is that Wren?" Not Cass, an older woman.

"Yeah. Who's this?"

"This is Jamie's mother, Kelly."

"Oh, hi, Mrs Whitson. What's up? My mam's not here now."

"It's okay. It was you I wanted to talk to."

"What can I do for you?"

"Have you seen Jamie at all?"

"Not since we went camping on Friday night," Wren replied, feeling a creeping foreboding climbing up to his shoulders. "Why, haven't you?"

"Not since Sunday. That's the last time anybody saw him. Sunday night."

"You rang around?"

"I've phoned everyone I could think of. You're the last." She sounded remarkably calm about it all. "Wren, he left the house without his shoes or his coat in the pouring rain."

Wren was silent for a short time, thinking frantically. "He probably had a borrowed pair on or something. The shoes."

"Do any of his friends have the same shoe size?"

Wren considered for a minute, adjusting his cap. Jamie's feet were huge. "Not even close."

"He's seemed very quiet ever since all this palaver about the Eastern Alliance began. I'm concerned he might have done something silly while he was upset." All delivered in that cut-glass, upper-class accent, in a purely informative tone. Wren had never liked her much, but he *really* disliked her now, because she seemed to care less than he did about her own son.

"Have you called the police?"

"Oh, I don't think it's quite come to that yet."

"Okay then. Well, I'll go and look for him, ask around."

"Would you? Thank you awfully."

"No problem. Bye."

"Goodbye."

Wren hung up and called the police. Ice Queen might not give a shit, but he did, and he knew what Jamie's depressions were like. Why hadn't the idiot given him a call instead of running off? He didn't seriously think Jamie was in trouble, probably hiding out at someone's house. Maybe his mother had already rung the house where he was staying, but Jamie had asked his host to lie for him. Wouldn't be the first time he'd tried to avoid his parents.

So why was he still standing here, with the receiver to his ear, on hold at the local missing persons' desk?

Because the whole world was going crazy, and as far as anyone being predictable was concerned, all bets were off.

He made the report to an uninterested police officer who evidently had heard it all before and was frankly bored with the prospect of chasing another disaffected kid. Once he'd put the phone down, he rang a few people who said they honestly *hadn't* seen Jamie. Mayner wasn't in, and nor was Kayleigh – not that he really wanted to speak to her after their argument.

He had just replaced the receiver and was about to go look for him at some of their old haunts, all business with Cass forgotten, when the doorbell rang. By the blobby patchwork of colours in the dimpled glass, he saw it was Kayleigh.

"I *so* don't need to deal with you right now," he muttered, going to open the door. But as he did so, any thoughts of resuming their previous argument faded. She leaped in through the door at him, face aglow, wearing a smile of such perfect happiness that she looked almost beatific.

She hugged herself to Wren so fiercely that she knocked the breath out of him, but he managed to put his arms around her, shutting the door on the outside world with one hand on the way.

"You heard from him?" he guessed, and the fresh hug that brought his ribs to cracking point told him he was right.

"They got him out," she said, the words coming out in a jumble. "He got airlifted. He called just now from Australia. . ." The last word dissolved into an incoherent shiver of sobs, as the release of all the pent-up emotion finally overwhelmed her.

He led her into the lounge and sat down with her on the sofa, holding her as she cried. His parents were at work, thankfully. He didn't want them around, asking her daft questions. Her tears dried quickly, pushed away by the happiness at the news of her father's survival. From the excited babble that poured from her, Wren gleaned that her father had been part of the defence force that was crushed beneath the first wave of Russian Federation forces that invaded the Philippines. He had been one of the few survivors, finding his way to the evacuation point and getting out before the islands were totally overcome. Only now had he reached safe haven, been debriefed and allowed to call his family.

"I should phone Mayner," she said breathlessly. "He came round just before we got the call. I was pretty upset . . . he might be worried."

Wren made a neutral noise, not really listening. He was caught up in himself. He could almost physically feel the lightening of the load on him. He hadn't noticed just how much Kayleigh's worry had weighed on him until it was gone. Sure, he'd cared about her father, but as he'd only met him once he had no real emotional connection. He cared because *she* cared, and he cared about her.

At last, something had gone *right*. But as he held her in his arms, he found that he couldn't be happy. There was something he had to tell her. Maybe before he would have hesitated, knowing how easily she might break if he handled her clumsily; but now her father had made contact, she was tough enough to take it.

"There's some bad news, Kayleigh," he said. She sat up away from him, as if stung that he could introduce such a subject in the midst of her ecstasy.

"What is it?" she asked.

"It's Jamie. He's missing."

"Missing?" she asked, cooling.

"Since Sunday," he replied.

Kayleigh was silent for a few moments. "So?" she said

almost snappishly. "He's gone off to stay with someone."

"Maybe. Nobody knows where he is, though. And apparently he left the house without his shoes."

"Is that significant?" Kayleigh asked. There was an edge to her tone that Wren didn't like. It was almost as if she was pissed at him for being inconsiderate enough to bring this up while she wanted to celebrate. *Her* worries had been resolved, so everyone else's could wait for a while.

"No shoes means nothing on his feet. It was raining. Any of this strike you as strange?" he said, his voice becoming a little harder in response. It occurred to Wren then that even in the midst of such great news as Kayleigh had just received, the two of them were *still* spoiling for a fight after yesterday's argument. There had to be something really wrong with that.

She didn't give him a reply to his question. He decided to let it go. For a short while, they sat in silence, tense, the previous joy having fled the room.

Is she what I really want? Wren thought, and blinked in surprise that it had even crossed his mind.

"I'm going on that march tomorrow," she said. "Stop the Countdown."

Wren hesitated. She was in an extremely volatile mood, and he had a habit of saying the wrong thing in such a situation. Unfortunately, the hesitation was all the excuse Kayleigh needed.

"You don't want me to go," she accused suddenly, glaring at him.

"Since when did I say that?"

"You didn't have to," she snapped.

"So basically I didn't say anything, and you made the rest up." He *hated* it when she guessed at his reactions. She was always wrong.

"Why don't you want me to go?" she persisted. "You think it's hopeless, right? You're so . . . you're so cynical, you won't even raise a finger to change what's going on."

"Will you get off this trip, Kayleigh? I don't care if you go on some rally."

"No, that's the point, you *don't* care."

Wren sighed, got up off the sofa and walked out into the kitchen. Kayleigh, after a moment, went after him. He was putting his shoes on.

"What the hell do you think you're doing?" she cried.

He straightened and looked at her. "I'm not having one of our stupid arguments, not now. One of those ones where you turn everything I say around and selectively forget bits of the conversation you can't use against me." He knew what this was about. It wasn't about the rally, or about Jamie. Kayleigh was still mad that he'd gone to see Cass. That was what was beneath it all, the unspoken spur. She was jealous. Well, he couldn't help that, and he wasn't going to spend hours arguing around the subject. He had more important things to do. He had to find his friend. "I'm going out. You can stay, if you want."

Kayleigh stared at him in disbelief. "Don't just *walk away* from me!" she howled.

"Know what? That's *exactly* what I'm gonna do." And

with that, he opened the front door and walked out into the dismal Tuesday afternoon. The sound of the door slamming behind him haunted him the rest of the day, while he was searching for Jamie. He kept on looking long after it had become useless, partly because of his concern for his friend, but mostly because he didn't want to go home and find the last bridge to Kayleigh a smoking char.

Night settled over Sheffield. The hillsides were studded with rows of streetlights, and lights glowed in the windows of houses. The Forte Posthouse hotel sign rose above it all like a beacon, and the multi-storey blocks of offices and university departments were dark, except for a few rooms on the upper floors where the lights never seemed to go off.

The temperature fell after midnight, until by two o'clock breath steamed in the air. In the city centre, several clubs were open and doing brisk business; people needed a release more than ever now, and there were innumerable fights and glassings. The police were kept busy.

But the affairs of the rest of Sheffield mattered nothing to Mayner. He was concerned with his own private task. Bundled up in his long snowboard jacket, he stood in the back garden of Kayleigh's house, looking up at her window, a shadow in the cold darkness.

His heart was thumping in his chest, hard enough for him to feel his pulse all over his body. He hadn't even done anything yet, but the simple fact of his presence in a friend's garden at night made him feel guilty. He was a trespasser, even though he would be in no real trouble if he was caught. Not while he was still out here. After all, Kayleigh knew him. She'd just think him a bit weird.

Yet he was still experiencing an unpleasant cocktail of fear, nervousness and shame. Because he knew what he was *about* to do.

He had waited there for a long time. Her back garden was screened in by a high fence, with a road running behind it. There was the occasional swoosh of a car passing in the night, the bright beam of headlights fanning through the narrow slats in the fence. The steady exhalation of the wind.

He drew Kayleigh's back-door key out of his pocket and let it rest in his palm, looking at it. The sight of it had the curious effect of numbing his fear. It said: *you've gone this far, it's too late now.*

Of course it wasn't too late. It wasn't too late when he'd called round to see Kayleigh, when he'd hung around awkwardly as she cried about her father and how she still hadn't heard from him, when he'd sneakily stolen the key from the hook on the way to the toilet. It wouldn't be too late until he stepped inside the house.

Or was he just kidding himself? Had it all been decided the moment he accepted Jester's hand, when the skinhead had helped him up after his last beating? And it really was his *last* beating.

Sod it, he thought. *You've chosen your path. Go through with it.*

His hand clasped on the key, and he walked across the garden towards the back door of the house. There was a moment when he paused, the tip of the key resting on the lower lip of the crooked slot, and his heartbeat suddenly seemed to jump to deafening volume in his ears. He took a sharp breath, feeling as if his entire body, his skin and his hair, was throbbing in sync with the pump in his chest. Lowering his head, he let it pass, listening as the sound gradually receded back to normal. For long moments, he stood there in the night, the key angled into the Yale lock; then he thrust it home, and slowly turned it to the side.

The door seemed to pop open as soon as the bolt had cleared the frame, sucking inwards with a sigh of air, inviting him into the darkness beyond. He could still close it now, could just turn and walk away, there was no need to do this. . .

He stepped inside before the doubts could get a grip, softly closing the door behind him. Cool blue shadows of a dim moon lay across the furniture, spreading languidly along the floor. He was in the back room, a kind of mini-lounge edged with bookshelves, where Kayleigh's parents would sit to read or entertain friends. Two small wicker sofas and a matching pair of easy chairs sat silent, the floral pattern on their cushions sharpened by the icy light.

He listened for a time, breathing softly, alert for any sound that might mean his intrusion had been noticed. Nothing, except the creaks and grumbles of the house as its boards and pipes settled in the night chill.

He walked across the room, every muscle in his body tense, and stepped through into the hallway. The moonlight glowed through the latticed window of the front door, illuminating the heavy banister of the stairs. Mayner found the empty hook by the downstairs bathroom, wiped the key on his coat sleeve and carefully replaced it. Probably nobody had even noticed it was gone. He—

Noises. He froze. A tinny tapping sound, rapid, rising and falling and—

Applause. There was a TV on somewhere.

He almost bailed out right at that moment. He had already retreated halfway across the back room again before he stopped himself.

It might have been left on. It might be a TV next door. Do you want to do this or don't you?

He did want to. More than anything, he wanted to go through with the plan of which this was only the first part. More than anything.

And he found himself turning around, walking back to the hall. And there, he listened. How many TVs were there? One upstairs in Kayleigh's room . . . one in the lounge . . . maybe one in her parents' room; he'd never been in there.

The one in the lounge. He could see now. The faint play of cathode ray light on the stippled glass of the lounge door, shifting randomly as the picture on the screen switched and changed. The TV was on, turned down quiet.

Had they just forgotten to turn it off? Doubtful. Had someone fallen asleep in front of it? Possible. Or was someone awake, maybe having a swift bout of insomnia, watching late-night trash to tide them over while they waited for tiredness to overtake them?

The latter was far more likely.

You can still do this. Just be quiet.

The lounge door was shut, but it was only thin glass set in a narrow frame. The stippling meant it was hard to see through; as he crept up and peered in, he could only see the faint smudge of the glowing TV in the darkness. All the other lights were out. Was there someone sitting with their back to him, watching the screen? He couldn't tell.

The door opposite led to Kayleigh's father's study, more sturdy wood. He clenched his fist hard enough to make his nails dig into his palm, and then stepped boldly over to it, quietly twisting the brass knob. The door opened with a faint *swoosh* as it dragged over the carpet; then he stepped inside and shut it behind him.

The dresser, by the window. The light on this side of the house was so meagre that he could hardly see, but he was guided by purpose now. He slid open the dresser drawer, lifting it slightly on its runners to minimize the noise. He reached inside.

There.

Slipping his prize into his coat pocket, he closed the drawer without a sound and returned to the door. Once more, opening the study door, stepping through and—

Son of a bitch! Someone was there, someone was there, someone was—

No, no, no. For the briefest of moments, he had thought that he had seen Kayleigh on the other side of the stippled glass of the lounge door, standing an inch from the glass, watching him. It was nothing. A trick of the unnatural light, a phantom of his own guilt. His heart slowly sank back into its rightful place.

Just get out of here, he thought to himself. He closed the study door without a sound, padded through to the back door, and turned the latch. Without a moment's hesitation, he slipped through and was free, pulling the door shut behind him with the softest of clicks.

CHAPTER NINE

"No, Jane, I think the only indication coming from NATO right now is that the situation is, if anything, getting worse. Violent protests, both for and against the war, have erupted all over the globe. Terrible rioting in Pakistan has led the government to declare a state of martial law across the entire country. Several African nations have erupted into civil war over disagreements about the invasion into Kenya and Somalia. The Prime Minister is calling for a global summit, to try and persuade the Eastern Alliance to halt their advance while a solution can be found to the impending Big Freeze. The President is saying that nothing less than a total withdrawal will be accepted, and that he is prepared to consider a nuclear option if that does not happen. NATO is in pieces, with all sides disagreeing, but one thing is certain: the deadline remains. And with less than forty-eight hours to go, only a last-minute *turnaround seems likely to stop the nations of Earth plunging into what may well be World War Three."*

"But surely that's terrifically counterproductive. Can anybody win in such a situation?"

"Well, yes, it is counterproductive. Even suicidal. Speculation offers two possibilities in the event of war. First, a nuclear exchange, which will plunge the Earth into winter and only hasten the Big Freeze. Second, a protracted land-war, which will take up all the resources of the participant countries and leave none to take preventative measures against the oncoming Ice Age. Both options are equally fatal. But this is a match of wills, a test of muscle, and with the egos of the two most powerful countries in the world at stake, nobody wants to back down. Critics are calling it the New Cold War, and this time around the name has a morbidly appropriate ring to it."

Wren's eyes flickered open to the sound of the doorbell downstairs. He half-considered getting it, then decided it wasn't important enough to get out of bed for, then remembered his mother was probably around anyway. The sound of the latch being turned back reassured him that the caller would not go ignored, and he drifted back towards sleep again, his preferred environment.

What seemed like a few seconds later – though it could have been an hour for all he knew – he was brought back to awareness by a soft knocking on his door.

"Yeah?" he said muzzily.

His mother pushed open the door a little and peeked her head through apologetically. "You awake, Andrew?"

"No, Mam," he said, gently sarcastic. "*You're* asleep, and you're only dreaming that I'm talking to you."

In the normal course of things, his mother would have matched him with a cutting comment, but this morning she only looked faintly distressed. If he could have seen her hands, he'd guess she would be wringing them right now.

"What's up?" he asked, brought fully awake by the unease on her face.

"The police are here, Andrew," she said.

He groaned. "What am I meant to have done?"

"It's not you, dear. It's about Jamie."

Wren met her eyes for a moment, then nodded slightly. "Can you give me a sec to get dressed?"

"Of course," she said, ducking out and closing the door.

He came downstairs a few minutes later, in his customary baggy clothes and reversed baseball cap, still smelling of sleep and with a pillow imprint in red on the side of his face. There was a policewoman waiting in the foyer, talking gravely with his mother.

"Andrew Wren?" asked the policewoman unnecessarily. "Sorry to get you up."

"S'alright," he said. She was slim, petite, short blonde hair, not attractive or unattractive but somewhere in between. The archetypal WPC.

"It's about your friend Jamie Whitson, who you reported missing yesterday."

"You found him?"

"Yes."

It was the way she said it, the fractional pause and flicker of the eyes, the slight moment of indecision as she calculated how to answer him. And the word, sympathetic and heavy at the same time.

He was dead.

The world seemed to thunder in on him, flapping and whirring around the edges of his vision like a frenzied flock of ravens. The blood drained out of his face and extremities, and a cold shroud seemed to settle on him. The policewoman could see by his reaction that he had guessed the news, and she lowered her eyes.

"I'm very sorry," she said.

His mam put an arm round him. "Oh, Andrew. . ."

"What happened?" he asked. It was a distant voice that spoke, an automatic question. He really didn't want to hear the answer, but his head was freewheeling and his mouth was trying to fill in the blanks.

"We don't know. He was found out in the countryside," the WPC said. She didn't seem to want to impart any more information than was necessary to Wren in his shocked state.

"What *happened*?" he repeated, a little more forcefully.

"Some ramblers found him in a ditch. We think he'd fallen asleep there. Nobody's certain what he was doing. He wasn't wearing any shoes, and he only had light clothes on. We don't have a coroner's report yet, but . . . well, it was probably either exposure or illness; something brought on by spending two nights in the

Peaks without any warm clothes. He was soaking wet."

"Okay," he said dully.

The WPC looked from one of them to the other. "We'll have to ask you some questions later, if that's alright. There's a lot of things we don't know about the circumstances. We'll call back in a few days."

"Thank you," said his mother, and the policewoman left, closing the door behind her.

Wren looked at the door for a moment, and then his mam hugged him. He gently pushed her off.

"Don't," he said quietly.

"Andrew, you're—" she began, but he cut her off.

"Just . . . don't," he whispered, and went upstairs to his room.

She brought him a cup of tea in the time-honoured tradition of English mothers, and then left him alone as he wanted. He didn't know it, but he was mimicking exactly what Jamie had been doing a few days earlier, lying on the bed, staring at the ceiling. The Get Up Kids were playing in the background, but they were just there to fill up the emptiness in the room.

Somewhere distant, a rally was gathering in the town centre. Kayleigh would be there. Mayner would probably be around. He wondered if they knew that Jamie had gone.

There was a void in his chest, a great mass of nothing where there should have been grief, anger, *anything*. Instead there was blankness.

He didn't see it coming. Why hadn't he *thought*? Everyone was strung out about the war, everyone was tied up with their own problems. He'd been thinking about Kayleigh and Cass; between them, he'd forgotten about Jamie.

Alone. He'd died in a ditch.

What the *hell*?

Wren could see it all. Whether he was right or wrong, it didn't matter. He could follow the logic in his mind, and it made enough sense to make sense.

We don't have any control! If the PM decides to start a war, he can come knocking on my door and make me go fight and kill in a country I never gave a shit about, he can destroy my life and everything I planned for, and I can't do a damn thing about it!

That was it. Jamie's words. He could recall them perfectly, could see the way his face moved and his glasses reflected the flames of the campfire as he talked. He had been unravelling even then, falling apart, and they hadn't seen it. He thought of Jamie's father, the strict military man with a heart of leather, and his distant mother, whose life was lived through manners, never touching on any deeper feelings. He wondered if they even looked up from their newspapers when they heard of Jamie's end.

Nobody to turn to. Not Mayner, who wouldn't understand. Not his parents, who'd be disappointed that he couldn't deal with it himself. Not Kayleigh, who had her own problems.

And not me, Wren thought. *Not me. You idiot, you stupid bastard, you could have come to* me!

This war, this bloody war . . . people even talked about it as if it was already happening. In everyone's mind, it had become inevitable. In everyone's mind, it had already started. It had already claimed someone close to him. What would happen now if the superpowers climbed down? What if there *was* no war? It was already too late for Jamie.

Is this how frail it all was? Is this how much it took to scrape the lacquer of civilization off humanity? The threat of a war?

No, not that. Humankind had been through wars before. It was the Big Freeze, the Ice Age. The Earth had betrayed them all, and the little ticks that lived on its surface were going into a frenzy. Somewhere, on some instinctive, animal level, they *knew*, each and every one, that a cataclysm was coming. And it frightened them, like thunder frightened the cavemen.

You dumb, desperate, misguided son of a bitch. Why did you do it?

The doorbell rang. He had no idea how long he'd been lying on his bed, but the bright sunlight outside was still strong. Maybe if the sun had been there yesterday, instead of hiding behind cold clouds, Jamie wouldn't be dead now.

His mother opened the door. Surprise in her voice, but he couldn't tell what was said. All he heard was, "He's in his room," at the end of their brief exchange. The creak of the stairs. Whoever it was, he didn't care. Unless it was Jamie.

It wasn't Jamie. It was Cass instead. She walked across the room and sat down on the bed next to him.

"I heard," she said.

Wren began to cry.

CHAPTER TEN

"Realistically, though Mr Chambers: what chance does an event like this – of whatever scale – have of changing the course that NATO have set?"

"Absolutely none at all. Jane, if every person in the British Commonwealth gathered in one spot and spelled out STOP THE COUNTDOWN in letters large enough to be seen from orbit, NATO would still ignore them. Apart from the loss of face and the humiliation, apart from the terrible atrocities that we would be permitting to happen by letting the Eastern Alliance continue their invasion, you must understand that bureaucracy is a very slow and lazy animal. Punch a dinosaur in the tail and it would take a while for the message to get to its brain. Magnify that by a hundred and you have NATO, or indeed any other international cooperative. It would take days for NATO to react to any kind of protest. Votes must be taken, procedure must be agreed. Only one thing can stop it in time: the Eastern Alliance agreeing to withdraw its troops."

"But isn't it too late by now? Wasn't the Eastern Alliance supposed to withdraw all its troops by the deadline? It would take at least a week to demobilize now, if not longer. They're already too firmly entrenched, surely."

"I think even a force as inflexible as NATO would prefer to play out some slack rather than start a World War. If the Eastern Alliance promises to withdraw – and they may well do, as a tactic to gain time – then the deadline will undoubtedly be set back. The pot will be taken off the boil for a short while. That doesn't necessarily mean the Eastern Alliance will make good on their promise; but it would certainly allow people to prise their fingers from their armrests long enough to make a cup of tea and reappraise the situation."

The people had gathered.

Not even the organizers had predicted how many would turn up in Sheffield city centre during the hours surrounding three pm on a hot Wednesday in July. Stop the Countdown had become an increasingly attractive prospect as the zero hour approached, a last stab at sanity, one chance to do what little they could to halt the destruction that was sure to come. The twenty-four-hour mark had ticked by at two pm that day. Less than twenty-four hours for the Eastern Alliance to give up their territories, or for NATO to back down – nobody really cared which, as long as it was one or the other. Less than twenty-four hours to avert another World War.

To Wren, the morning had seemed to last for ever. It seemed like he had been awake for days. He had crushed so much grief and emotion into such a short space of time that the minutes had stretched to accommodate him.

Jamie was dead. News travelled fast along the grapevine. But his death had brought Cass.

Her arrival had been too much. Wren wept like a baby for hours, both for Jamie and for what he had done to Cass, for the lost year and a half that he had not dared to face up to. He didn't deserve to know her, this girl that could shovel aside all the pain of her own mother's death to comfort him when he was in mourning. And while he was at his lowest ebb, with nothing else to lose in terms of pride, he told her everything: about how much of a coward he had been, how he felt about Michiko and what he had done to her, how much he hated himself for losing Cass when she was the best thing he'd ever had.

And as he spoke, a fractured stream of consciousness, he purged himself, retching up rancid clots of emotion that had weighed down on his gut for too long now. Truths poured out of him that he had not even admitted to *himself*, dangerous and inappropriate but unstoppable anyway. How he had loved her, and how it had destroyed him to lose her that way. How he still missed her after all this time. And how inexpressibly, utterly *sorry* he was for what he had done.

She hardly spoke, only held him and listened. What effect his words had on her, he could not tell. She simply let him talk, without interruption or reaction; and eventually, his confessions ran dry, and he began to think of what he had yet to do.

"We have to tell them," he said. "We've gotta go find Kayleigh and Mayner, tell them about Jamie. We can't wait till tonight. There isn't time." He didn't need to spell out why. The clock was ticking inside all of their heads, and nobody could now deny the very real fear that there would be no last-minute backdown.

He could hardly breathe. It was more than a sensation of claustrophobia, the walls closing in on him. More than even the entire *city* crowding close. It was time itself that was boxing him in. He could not even afford the luxury of grief, when all he wanted to do was lie in bed for ever and not move an inch for anyone. Two spins of the hour hand was all he might have left. There was so much to be done, so many things left unsaid.

"We'll find them," Cass said. "If we're meant to find them, things will fall that way."

Cass had always been a firm believer in fate, that everything followed some kind of plan. She ignored the odds of finding one girl in many thousand. If fate decreed that they should find Kayleigh and Mayner, then the odds meant nothing.

Wren had recovered himself a little by the time they went out. He assured his mother he was okay, that Cass would look after him. She glanced at Cass with a look that suggested she wasn't sure. She knew about her son and Michiko, and was frankly worried about leaving Wren with Cass while he was in such a raw and vulnerable state. Who knew what damage she could do if she tried?

In the end, she kept her protests to herself.

Despite the urgency, they walked slowly into town. Wren needed to compose himself a little. His tears had dried, and no real trace remained, but he was still fragile, and he didn't know if he could handle the crowds.

The crowds, as it turned out, were bigger than he imagined. Traffic had ground to a halt, and several cars that had been unwise enough to brave the town centre were stranded like islands in the sea of people. Outside the City Hall, the ornamental gardens were buried under a blanket of chattering faces. Everywhere, there was a crush, and only at the very edges of the pavement where they ran up against the shop fronts could anyone move without having to jostle and push. Banners rose above the throng, bearing slogans: some professionally printed and others hand-made. An enormous, tapestry-sized banner hung between the pillars of the enormous building, declaring the intention of the rally: STOP THE COUNTDOWN! A podium stood beneath it, flanked by the massive speakers of a PA system.

Wren and Cass skirted the edges of the main mass, looking about for signs of Kayleigh or Mayner. Cass had absently taken his hand to prevent them getting separated, but Wren found himself getting distracted by it, his thoughts constantly turning to the feel of her skin on his instead of concentrating on the task of finding the others.

But there were just too many people. And after a

quarter of an hour, they still had not covered even a fraction of the crowd; even then, the chances were that they wouldn't have seen either Kayleigh or Mayner. Mayner was short anyway, and Kayleigh, while tall for a girl, was still not *that* tall.

They were still hustling when a swift whine of feedback indicated that the PA system had been turned on and the rally was about to begin. Wren glanced at Cass's watch. Three o'clock.

"*People of Sheffield!*" came the cry. It was a woman, but Wren couldn't see the podium from where he was. The crowd roared in response, a surge of noise with an almost breathless power behind it.

"*Thank you all for coming! There are more of you here than anyone could have guessed! Let's hope this sends a message, a message to the people in power who are playing with our lives! Stop the countdown!*"

Another roar, even louder than the last.

Wren and Cass exchanged a glance. She smiled and squeezed his hand, seeing the slight worry on his face. The crowds were beginning to freak him a little. It was frightening how easily they had slipped back into the familiarity of being with each other, even with all that was left hanging unresolved between them.

He looked away after a moment to resume his search, and a fleeting frown crossed his brow. Was that . . . no, he was gone. For a moment, he thought he'd seen the now-familiar skinhead/bomber jacket combination of the UKCDF. They had become an increasingly common sight over the last few days.

What were they doing here, though?

"Hey, there she is," Cass said, tugging at him. "Told you we'd find her."

She was right. There was Kayleigh's distinctive blonde tresses, a short way in front of them. She was clapping above her head and cheering as the speaker continued. Wren let go of Cass's hand and began to make his way through the shoulders of the crowd to get to her, carving a path for Cass to follow. Luckily, Kayleigh was not near the centre of the gathering, where the crowd would be far too thick to push through.

She turned at his touch, her face lighting into a smile as she saw him . . . and then falling as her eyes passed to Cass.

"And what is *this*?" she said, wariness and anger in her tone.

"Listen, Kayleigh, I've got to tell you something," Wren said, being jostled from one side as someone else pushed past him. He was about to speak again, but the words hitched in his throat and tears threatened.

"What is *she* doing here?" Kayleigh asked, ignoring what he had just said.

"It isn't what you think," Cass said, bristling slightly because she was being referred to in the third person, as if she wasn't there at all.

"*It is our responsibility,*" the speaker came over the PA in the background, "*our duty to our children to stop the powermongers who think that war is an answer. Don't they learn? Hasn't every war only brought suffering and misery? When will we realize that war is the final failure of civilization? That violence is no solution at all but an admission that we are still animals? Let's show them, here, that we can use the power of peace to change our lives."*

"And what *do* I think?" Kayleigh said, rounding on Cass. "Where did you come from, anyway? What are you doing with my boyfriend?"

"Kayleigh, forget it for the moment, I've got something more important—" Wren began, but she wouldn't be stopped now.

"No, I won't *forget* it! I'd like a straight answer, if it's not too much trouble, me being your girlfriend and all."

"Will you stop being so damn petty for a minute?" Wren cried. "I told you I—"

"Oh, is this being petty to you? You know, it seems—"

"*Jamie's dead!*" he shouted into her face, his frayed nerves snapping. "*Do you get that? Can you hear me? He's bloody dead!*"

The flame seemed to go out of Kayleigh for a moment, snuffed by the news. She seemed to diminish a little, shrinking back. The people next to them in the crowd were desperately pretending not to have heard them.

"I just wanted to tell you, that's all," Wren said; and suddenly he didn't want to be around her any more, he didn't want to have to deal with her. It seemed absurd to care about something so petty in the face of the crisis that loomed, but it occurred to him then that he was really thinking about *leaving* her, not just right then but for ever. Breaking up. Were the arguments really worth the good times in between? Could he even be bothered to take it any more?

Or was he just running out on another girlfriend in her time of need?

"Wren!" she called after him, but he was already going. Cass went with him. Kayleigh didn't.

Mayner had other things on his mind than being at the rally. He only cared about Stop the Countdown insofar as it provided a welcome distraction from the business he was about. Most people were either there or listening to it on the radio. The police would have their eyes on it, and would be paying scarce attention to anything else. Good.

Stop the Countdown. What a daft idea. As if anything *could* stop it now.

Mayner had made his choices. Without even realizing it, he had given himself up to the idea that everything was going to end tomorrow afternoon, two o'clock pm GMT. Not *literally*, no. But one way or the other, everything he knew was going to be destroyed. Whether they went to war, whether they were nuked off the planet, it didn't matter. Nothing could stop it. And nobody would care about anything else. They especially wouldn't care about Tracksuit and Slacks.

Mayner sat, and waited, and let his hand rest on the cool metal of the snub-nosed revolver in the pocket of his Billabong jacket.

He'd known where Kayleigh's father kept the gun. They all knew. He'd been round her house enough times; after all, she had been one of their circle of friends for years. Kayleigh's father was a soldier; it was in his disposition to have the means to defend himself.

So he kept a loaded handgun in the dresser drawer in his study. Probably had one upstairs, too, but Mayner didn't know about that. As Kayleigh had grown up, her father had lost the habit of locking the drawer. Lucky for Mayner.

He had been in and out of the house in two minutes flat. No evidence of a burglary, except for the missing gun. And who'd want to break in just to steal a revolver? What were the chances of them checking, anyway?

He was sweating under his heavy coat. It was a hot day, the sun riding high and bright as if to make up for the recent rain. He was sitting on a wall next to a bus shelter. On the other side of the road was a line of houses. A railway line ran to the back of him, surrounded by scrubland cluttered with junk.

He couldn't say what it was about the UKCDF that appealed to him, but it was that manifesto that had snared him. Wren had been typically sceptical about it, but then Mayner and Wren disagreed on a lot of things. And it wasn't that Mayner gave a shit about defending his country, or any of that. It was just the tone of the thing. It was about strength, union, solidarity. Alone, he wasn't strong enough to defend himself against his enemies. That gave him two choices if he wanted to better himself; either find friends that were, or *make* himself strong enough.

Mayner was sick of being down. Sick, sick, more than he could possibly have believed. So sick that fear seemed weak in comparison. The last of it had fallen away from him as he left Kayleigh's house. Power was there for those who had the guts to take it. He wasn't talking about megalomania, no Bond villain stuff . . . just the power to make his own life liveable again. The power to take control.

That was what he saw when he read the UKCDF manifesto that Jester had given him outside the school. The patriotic stuff just glanced off him, but the underlying message stuck. If you want to defend yourself, you have to be ready to fight. If you want to fight, *arm* yourself.

For the first time, he had found something approaching an answer. But that was as far as it had gone. He had no love for the UKCDF or their kind, even though he happened to agree with some of their opinions. Until that moment when Jester had turned up, his Desert Eagle in his hand, and saved him from the kicking he had been promised by Tracksuit and Slacks.

Unlike Cass, Mayner didn't believe in fate. In truth, he'd never really thought about it. It was just coincidence to him that Jester was there; the skinhead said later that he'd remembered Mayner's face from the school, because he'd seemed interested. Just happened, is all.

When Jester asked him to come by to a meeting the next day, it seemed the least he could do after the skinhead had pulled him from the fire. He promised to come, and he stuck to it. They met at Jester's flat, a small, neatly-maintained place which was plastered with home-made UKCDF propaganda. The other guys there were rough but friendly in a comradely sort of way. They commiserated with him on his many bruises, and said they'd help him out with any payback that they could.

Payback. Now *that* was something Mayner was desperate to get hold of. And so they talked, and he was surprised at the willingness of these strangers to listen to his problems. They treated him like one of their own almost immediately. They respected him for his anger, instead of dismissing it or trying to calm him.

It would be an initiation, they said. Do this, get your payback, and we'll let you in. It's your duty to beat your enemies, just like it's Britain's duty to destroy those who oppose it.

So Mayner sat, and waited, watching the house across the road. It hadn't been hard to find the place; a friend of a friend had told him where it was. The occupant was fairly well known and loathed locally.

Occasionally he brushed his fingertips across the cold metal of the gun in his pocket. He'd been there since seven o'clock that morning.

Tracksuit couldn't hide in there for ever.

The police were at the rally, of course. Any gathering of that size required their presence. Plain-clothes officers moved between the crowds, while the more conspicuous uniformed ones hung round the edges. They knew well enough how easily something like this could get out of control. It had been happening all over the world. People were scared, and scared people got angry, and angry people got violent. Especially in crowds. It just took a spark to be thrown, and that would be it.

While Mayner waited outside Tracksuit's house with a snub-nose revolver, Jester and his companions were at the peace rally, throwing sparks.

It was a remarkably organized effort. The UKCDF had contacts in many other, similar organizations. They knew the professional rabble-rousers, the hard core of the football hooligans, who made it their business to set off particularly volatile crowds. They knew the other Nationalist groups, who shared their beliefs. They wanted a war because they wouldn't stand for letting the Eastern Alliance threaten northern Australia, as it was a Commonwealth territory. And they knew the disaffected kids who were frightened out of their wits by the prospect of impending conflict and just wanted a fight to let off steam.

It started small. The trick was to sucker the police into starting something, make it look like it was their fault. A few guys started up a chant, "Screw-the-*pigs*, screw-the-*pigs*," on the edges on the crowd, and pretty soon others had taken it up. The police were the closest thing to authority figures that anyone had to hand, and that made them targets. People – mainly kids at first, but spreading steadily up the age range – began to get distracted from the rally and pay attention to the more exciting pastime of haranguing cops. The police, in turn, began to get nervous and call in for reinforcements; which was exactly what the agitators wanted them to do. It was turning into a face-off, police against the public.

By the time the riot police arrived, stones and assorted junk were being thrown at the regular constabulary. One of the UKCDF lobbed a Molotov cocktail that emerged from his bag, deliberately pitched so it wouldn't hit anyone, only scare them. The bottle burst in a pool of flame, and the riot police surged forward, seeing the danger. The crowd interpreted it as an attack, and the counter-assault began.

More riot police arrived, on other sides of the city centre, to contain the trouble if it spread. Their presence was sufficient cause for some of the more volatile sections of the crowd to begin shouting abuse, and the cycle started again.

In less than an hour, several sections of the immense crowd, separated by streets and shops and office buildings, had degenerated into battle. Running fights were conducted down alleys. Riot police formed barricades with their toughened-plastic shields. Helicopters flew overhead, telling the crowd to disperse. Nobody did. The speaker on the podium began to heckle the police for trying to take away their freedom of speech.

The cancer was spreading, and its touch brought chaos.

CHAPTER ELEVEN

"Less than twenty-four hours until the NATO deadline expires, and the Eastern Alliance have as yet given no indication that they intend to go along with the demands. Attempts have been made to bring the leaders of both parties to the conference table, but NATO reports that all attempts at diplomacy have been ignored or politely turned aside. A spokesman said today that an official declaration of war would be made at two o'clock Greenwich Mean Time unless the Eastern Alliance offered full and unconditional compliance with NATO's conditions. Critics have demanded that NATO give up on what they are calling a 'face-off between the two neighbourhood bullies', arguing that a war would divert the country's resources and leave us unprepared for the Big Freeze when it hits. NATO have declared that there is no question of backing down. The Eastern Alliance's seizure of the equatorial countries is, to

their eyes, a monstrous impingement on human rights. Further speculation has been made in the Press concerning NATO's real motives. A columnist in the Times *has suggested that NATO are only angry that the Eastern Alliance got to the fertile land first; and a war is NATO's excuse for taking it all and sharing it with no one. Certainly, it explains why NATO chose to involve themselves in a conflict that they had no business interfering with. He ended his column with the same words with which I shall end my report: 'If you believe in a benevolent God, pray to him now, because only a miracle is going to avert World War Three at this point.'"*

Mayner jerked awake, almost falling off the wall.

"You getting on or what?" came a voice. He looked up, realizing that he must have slipped into a doze, and saw a bus waiting at the stop in front of him. The door was open, and the driver was leaning towards him from his cab, watching him expectantly.

"Oh. . ." he said blearily. "No, sorry mate."

The driver tutted, pulled the lever to close the door and drove away. Mayner watched it go, then returned to his vigil. Sweat had caked all over his body, and he felt grimy. Bloody coat, should never have brought it on a day like this. He—

The door to Tracksuit's house was opening.

Mayner swore, simultaneously thanking his luckies for the bus driver waking him up and feeling the cold wash of action pump through his tired body. Ducking around the edge of the shelter, he put graffiti-strewn metal between him and Tracksuit's door, so that he could watch without being seen.

It *was* Tracksuit. About time.

Mayner's hand unconsciously stole into his pocket to check that the gun was there. He wasn't exactly clear on what he was going to do, only that he was going to do *something*.

He watched his target slouch down the road, heading towards the city centre. He turned down a stone jetty and was gone. Mayner glanced either way for traffic and then followed him.

He was incredibly calm about it all. His heart wasn't even beating fast. Perhaps because he really, honestly didn't care any more. About anything. If he was going out, he wasn't going out without giving Tracksuit a taste of his own medicine. Slacks would come later.

Into the jetty, and there was Tracksuit at the end, in his trainers and his white outer skin. Did he ever *change*? Mayner walked brazenly after him, confident that Tracksuit wouldn't turn round and look behind, not really bothered if he did. What did it matter? What could happen that wouldn't be erased by this time tomorrow? What did the giants of the world care about the affairs of the insects?

Out on to another street, still within the depressing urban districts which even the bright, cheery sun could not make pleasant. Without realizing it, Mayner was synchronizing his own footsteps with Tracksuit's, as if to disguise his presence. His eyes were fixed on the back of his target's head, where the limp, greasy hair came to a point at the nape. He was sweating and red, but it was the heat and not the exertion or even the thrill. Inside, he was ice-calm.

Tracksuit turned on to a small park – more a wide patch of grass – and began walking across it. A few kids were playing football nearby, shouting "Penno!" every time one of them tackled and then arguing where the penalty spot was.

Now was as good a time as any.

"Hey! Tracksuit!" he called. It was the first time he'd referred to the guy by his nickname aloud, and it sounded curiously fitting. To most people, he'd have thought it an insult to refer to them by the clothes they wore; but for this one, it was just right.

Tracksuit responded to the tone, if not the content, of the hail. He turned around slowly, with an expression on his face that clearly said: *Come on then, if you think you can take me*. It changed to faint surprise when he saw who it was calling him. He looked past Mayner, suspicious, expecting to see more people about. If the kid had come for revenge, he'd bring a gang. But they were standing in the middle of open ground.

"What d'*you* want?" he asked belligerently.

Mayner didn't reply. Just carried on walking towards him.

Tracksuit appeared a little unnerved. This kid, four years younger and probably a good eight inches shorter than him, was displaying absolutely no fear at all. He didn't think it in that way – he didn't understand why the little sod was freaking him – but the effect was the same. Needing to restore some control, he sneered:

"Not been taught to talk yet? You had a pretty good mouth on you last time."

And then it occurred to him. He was thinking of the *second*-last time. The *last* time, someone had turned up with a gun. He felt suddenly afraid. Mayner saw the flash cross his face, and in a moment he had the revolver out, levelled at his enemy.

"*Shit!* What you doin' with that?" he said, backing away.

"Stay *right* there," Mayner said. He could hear the excited babble of the football kids as they spotted him. Tracksuit stopped his retreat. "Get down. On your knees."

It was as if Mayner was operating on automatic, following a script written for him by someone else. He knew exactly what he had to do. He was completely calm.

Tracksuit stood there, indecision freezing him. The football kids were mesmerized by the gun, whispering excitedly to each other.

"On your knees, you deaf bastard," Mayner said.

"What you gonna do?" Tracksuit asked, a wheedling tone in his voice beneath the aggressiveness. He was afraid to kneel, because that would be putting himself utterly in Mayner's power. He was just as afraid to stand.

"Nothing you don't deserve twice over," said Mayner. "Get *down!*"

Tracksuit knelt, slowly and reluctantly. "Look, mate, it was . . . we were just messing around."

"Really? Didn't feel like messing around."

In one swift movement, Mayner reversed the gun in his hand and smashed the butt of it across Tracksuit's face. Blood sprayed from Tracksuit's nose amid the nauseating crunch of gristle as it was crushed. He cried out in surprise; it took a moment for the pain to overtake the shock, but when it did he began to whimper, his hands coming up to cover his injury.

"Kinda felt like *that*," Mayner said.

It was wonderful. The feeling of utter *power*, that he had Tracksuit completely and totally in his control. Intoxicating. He could do anything, it seemed. The calmness had been replaced by euphoria and then, as he looked back at Tracksuit kneeling before him, a sudden overwhelming rage. In his mind, Tracksuit had become every kid who had punched, kicked, and bullied him in his life, spilt his Coke, made him carry their bag. Everyone who had kept him down, because he was small, because he seemed to go through life with a sign that said "TARGET" on his back and he didn't know why. All the frustration and unfairness was focused down to that moment, and on Tracksuit.

Mayner went berserk. He brought the butt of the gun down on the crown of Tracksuit's head, then lashed it across his cheek, feeling bone and teeth break. Tracksuit screamed, but Mayner was beyond sympathy. Face red and teeth gritted, he ploughed blows into the cringing form before him. One of the kids who had been playing football was crying in the background, but Mayner couldn't hear it over the whine of blood in his ears. His skin was hot, as if the fury inside him was literally burning; he thought of nothing but the thump-

thump-thump of the gun crashing down on Tracksuit's head, face and arms. In some distant part of himself, he was aware that he had lost it completely; but the voice of that part was too feeble to be heard over the animal bellow of his anger.

But Tracksuit wasn't done. His own pain and fear had panicked him, and he lashed out unexpectedly, suddenly launching himself into Mayner and bearing him to the ground. Mayner was taken by surprise, going down in a bundle of arms, and he felt a white explosion of pain as Tracksuit headbutted him in the face.

"Stop that! Oi, you two! Stop it!" someone was screeching. Sounded like a woman, but Mayner couldn't see where she was. He could only see Tracksuit's blood-smeared face, a dark domino-mask bruise around his eyes, his nose a broken wodge and his jaw dented. Spittle flew from his swollen lips as he pounded on Mayner, and Mayner struggled to get out from beneath him, and where the hell was the *gun*, anyway?

The report of the revolver was earsplitting, even muffled as it was between their bodies.

Oh, thought Mayner numbly. *There it is.*

Tracksuit had gone still, and a warm wetness was spreading across Mayner's chest. The gunshot echoed away into the silence that had suddenly fallen.

The kid who had been crying had stopped. The woman, whoever she was, had gone quiet. Mayner heaved Tracksuit off him, rolling him on to his back, and got up, the revolver still in his hand. He looked down at his enemy. The white tracksuit was bloodied and torn. A bullet hole in his torso was leaking red. His mangled face was an unrecognizable mess.

The moment stretched out for ever.

Mayner let the gun slip from his fingers, ran his hand gently over his newly-bruised face, and then turned and slowly walked away.

"Wren!" Cass cried, as the surge of people boiled up between them and pushed them apart. She reached for him, but her hand was knocked away by someone's shoulder.

The roar of the crowd pummelled their ears from all around, an incoherent tide of hollers and half-made words that formed the backcloth to the chaos all around them. Everywhere, men and women were shouting, their faces rendered ugly by aggression. Young children cried or hugged close to their mothers. People fought to get out in any direction, heading for where the crowd would be thinner; but movement was impossible. They could only go where the surge of bodies took them, and fighting against the flow was more than any single person had strength for.

Wren made to shout a response, but the crowd heaved again and suddenly someone was falling into him. He was toppling, his legs being buckled sideways and his hands reaching out in desperation to catch something. He caught a hand, but a quick snap shook him off and he went down, collapsing into the horde. His fall pushed a middle-aged man off his feet, and in a single, panic-filled moment seven people collapsed on top of each other, and Wren thrashed under the sudden, suffocating weight.

GetoffmegetoffmegetOFF

He'd fallen in a crowd several times before, mainly at gigs when he was dancing to a band. There was a certain unspoken crowd etiquette, even in the midst of immense gatherings like Glastonbury or Reading; if someone fell, you helped them up. The crowd would draw back in a circle to give them space to get to their feet again. Even in the dead centre of a crowd of forty thousand or so, the ritual was observed.

Not this time, however.

The crowd closed around them, someone *stepped* on his *back*, and he couldn't breathe. He flailed wildly, terrified, *ohGodohGodpleasedon'tletthisbeit*, and then suddenly his feet found stable ground and he surged upward, powering the people aside who lay scrabbling across him, and rising to his full height. The relief that flooded him was breathtaking; but he had only a moment to indulge, before he reached down and clamped his arm around a wild-eyed teenage girl, pulling her up and steadying her. He shoved angrily at the backs of the people who were stepping over those who had fallen; by that time, the middle-aged man that Wren had knocked down had gained his feet. Between them, they pulled the remaining people out of the trample zone, and they were safe again.

Or as safe as was possible, trapped in the midst of a riot.

Wren felt a hand grab his elbow roughly, and looked

back to see Cass reaching through the crowd for him. He barged his way through a gap that opened between them, and then he was at her side, pressed close to her by the crowd.

"What's happened?" she asked, her dark and frightened Oriental eyes searching his face.

"I dunno," Wren replied. "Let's get out of here."

There had been no warning that either of them could see. Deep in the heart of the rally, they had no idea of the conflicts going on around the fringes. Even when the helicopters started buzzing overhead, tinny voices telling them to disperse to their homes; even then, they had no idea about the violence that was to follow. The speaker at the podium started to make some oration about freedom of speech, and then suddenly the cheers turned ugly, shifting from yells of support to ones of hate and aggression towards the police. It was difficult to see anywhere over the crowd, especially as Wren was less than tall; but he almost *sensed* the riot sweep over them like a shockwave in reverse, spreading from the edges inward, with the epicentre being the City Hall.

It took only a tiny push to flip a gathering of this size into panic and anger, especially with the doom that hung over their heads. Wren wasn't sure what had set it off, and he didn't care. All that he was concerned about was getting him and Cass out of there.

And Kayleigh . . . what about Kayleigh?

She was out of his reach now.

He held Cass close to him with one arm and used his other to shove and push, hefting the human obstructions out of his way. His squat body gave him a deceptive strength, and his determination made him callous. He forced his way through the smallest gaps, with scarce thought as to who he was barging aside, thinking only of escape.

He glanced back once at Cass, and she gave him a brave smile, scared as she was. And even in the frantic crush of the riot, he felt a warm melt inside him at the sight, the first smile he'd seen from her in a year and a half.

It was difficult to tell how long they pushed and shoved, joining the throngs of people who were battling to get away, fighting against those who wanted to stay and vent their fear and hate on everyone around them. The helicopter was swooping overhead, urging the crowd to disperse in an infuriatingly calm tone.

What d'you think I'm trying *to do, you pack of shagwits?* Wren thought angrily.

They made their way towards the periphery of the crowd again. He kept his eyes fixed on a tall spire for navigation, heading in the direction that he was pretty sure would take them out of the centre and away from the riot. It was because he was so intent on that point that he didn't see the bottle arcing through the air towards him, spinning lazily in the air until it dashed against his head with a surprisingly soft tinkle. But whatever it sounded like, it *felt* like a sledgehammer, and Wren collapsed, boneless, into the dark.

...

...

...?

"Get out of my *way*! He's hurt!"

It was the distress in Cass's voice that slid him back into full consciousness. His face was wet and sticky, and his skull felt like a blast-quarry while the workers were dynamiting. A vague realization of what must have happened seeped into his brain; not the specifics, just the knowledge that he'd been hit on his head and that wet stuff on his face was probably, yes, blood.

He opened his eyes just as Cass cried out, and he was falling again. It was only at that moment that he realized the distant jogging-dragging sensation he had been feeling had been Cass carrying him, hefting his not-inconsiderable weight through the crowds by supporting him across the shoulders. But now that support was gone, and the moment of alarm as he crumpled blew away the last of the sparkling cobwebs across his mind.

"It's *your* damn fault he's hurt! Your sodding Chink mates!" came the reply, and then a swift thud followed by a yelp of pain from Cass.

Wren wiped the blood from his eyes – it *was* blood, and it was gushing pretty bad – and looked up. Somehow he'd lost his cap, and his short blond hair was stained red and matted to his scalp. He was lying on the ground, with Cass next to him, surrounded by the crowd. Three or four skinheads – UKCDF, undoubtedly, including the one that Mayner knew as Jester – were standing over them.

It took him a moment to calculate what had just happened, to put the sounds to the pictures. One of them had just thrown Cass and him to the ground and *kicked* her.

His eyes darkened in sudden fury. With a lurch, he got unsteadily to his feet and shoved the skinhead hard in the chest. His target tripped backwards and collapsed against one of his mates, who stopped him from falling.

"She's *Japanese*, you stupid bastards!" he shouted, his throat gone strangely dry. He lifted her up and got her to her feet. She was holding back sobs of shock and pain, but she stood. Wren glared at them balefully. "God, you guys are too thick to even manage being racist properly."

That was it. He knew that to provoke them was insane, but the thought of one of them swinging his boot into the girl at his side incensed him beyond reason. They piled into him, shoving Cass aside, four of them. He landed a punch on the one that had kicked Cass as they rushed him, getting him square on the jaw and knocking him near to senseless; but the other three tackled him to the ground, and suddenly he was in the midst of a forest of legs. All around him, people were still fighting or shouting or milling about, trying desperately to escape the crush, and he was buried under them.

The UKCDF had lost their bearings in the chaos of the fall; they had only meant to knock him down, but they ended up going down on top of him, pushed by a surge in the crowd. Somehow he scrabbled free. Someone hooked their arms under his shoulders and lifted him to his feet. "You gotta get to a hospital, mate," they said as they pulled him up, no doubt referring to the mask of blood that dribbled down his face from his scalp.

He ignored the well-meaning helper, instead stepping past his fallen enemies and trying to make his escape with Cass. Even as mad as he was, he wasn't going to kick them when they were on the floor. Tempting, but no.

The fourth skinhead was there, the one that he had lamped before. He had kept his feet, and now he swung a punch across Wren's face, surprising him. The blow didn't hurt as much as stun him, but Cass yelled and threw herself at his attacker, stamping on the back of his knees. He buckled, falling forward and down into Wren's uppercut, which caught him on the jaw again. Slumping down into the tangle of arms and legs, he lay still.

But the other three skinheads were up now, having forced their way to their feet. There was no way out; the crowd around them was too thick. Jester wiped his hand across his face and jabbed a finger at him.

"You're dead, mate."

And then the siren began.

It was a plaintive, distant noise, drifting out over the city like the cry of a mourning banshee. Soft-edged, yet loud. Ethereal yet unutterably sinister. It chilled where it touched, and those it chilled it froze, and thousands of people waited to hear what it might mean, what it *had* to mean.

"We're *all* dead, *mate*," Wren replied with a voice like a rusted knife.

CHAPTER TWELVE

"*This is a recorded broadcast. It will run every two minutes on this station until normal service can be resumed. A tactical nuclear strike has been launched by the Eastern Alliance upon those NATO countries with nuclear capability. Several dozen missiles are targeted towards England. Sheffield is the likely destination for several of these. Find shelter where you can. Underground locations, tunnels, bunkers, bomb shelters, are the most likely to ensure your survival. Do not panic. Cover any open shelter over with several feet of soil and planks. Be aware of the possibility of fall-out, and act in accordance with the procedures outlined in the pamphlets that were distributed to your homes and schools last week. Relief teams will be arriving as soon as possible. Stay tuned to this station. This is a recorded broadcast. It will run every two minutes until. . .*"

The streets were empty.

The evening sun spread a soft, warm light over the streets of Sheffield, casting long beams of orange-yellow glow between the shoulders of the buildings. Birds chimed and chattered in the trees, or swooped in the cloudless sky. The light wind stirred paper cups, streamers and beer cans, sending dog-ends of cigarettes scampering towards the gutters.

In the city centre, no one remained. Only the litter was left behind, torn buttons and splashes of drying blood, lost change and scorch-marks, a few overturned cars and a multitude of smashed windows.

The announcement had been made shortly after the siren began. The Eastern Alliance had decided to pre-empt the war and get their retaliation in first. A brace of missiles had been launched towards England, ETA unknown. Nukes. Britain had already responded with what little capability it had; the USA had done the same on a much larger scale. World War Three had begun. It would be the shortest war in what was left of history.

Nobody needed to be told what it meant. They had been educated enough in the last week to know what was going to happen. There were enough skyborne nukes winging their way across the globe to annihilate most of the world's major cities. The resulting dust cloud would blanket the Earth, plunging the survivors into a nuclear winter where nothing would grow, temperatures would plummet, and the sun would become a faint, hazy disc in a black sky.

And just as violence and anger had spread across the many thousands who were gathered in Sheffield for the Stop the Countdown rally, so did the eerie sense of calm that took over. Just as a rabbit will go limp in a dog's jaws as it realizes its life is over, so the people of Sheffield stopped their fighting. The raw shock had snuffed the flame of their anger.

They were witnessing the end of the world.

It took a few minutes for it to sink in. Then, slowly, people began drifting away, their improvized weapons dropping from limp hands. Dead-eyed, their faces stricken, they looked like the survivors of a plane crash as they stumbled away from the wreckage of their lives and back to their homes, their families. Like sleepwalkers, like zombies, they left the city centre. Even the riot police went, their jobs meaningless now. The soft *whup-whup-whup* of the helicopters faded as they headed off.

Within an hour, there was not a single person on the streets, and the riot was just a fading memory. There was only the faint bass hum of the PA system that had not been turned off, and the debris and destruction all around.

And there was Wren and Cass, walking on a small, flat park that stood at the juncture of several roads, just off West Street and near the Forum. A few trees rustled above them, the flat sides of their leaves sheening gold in the sun. Wren had washed the worst of the blood off his face in a fountain, and the gashes beneath his head had clotted to some extent. Mercifully, the cuts had not been deep; and they had bled out quickly, as head wounds do. His skull still thumped, but he didn't care any more. Of course he didn't care. He had perhaps only minutes left to live.

There was no point in running. No point in taking shelter. By some unspoken mutual consent, they had stayed when the others had gone. To meet the bull head-on. To be with each other.

"You know, I never thought we'd do it," said Cass, her voice steady. She had been crying earlier, but now she was almost serene. "I never thought mankind would really. . ." She trailed off.

"I always thought we would," said Wren. "I just didn't want to be around when I was proved right."

Cass smiled faintly. God, she was beautiful when she smiled.

"It's . . . I don't know, Wren. I don't know what I imagined it would feel like, but it wasn't like *this*."

Wren didn't reply. He just looked at her, watching her face as she spoke. After a moment she caught him, and smiled again.

"What?"

"Nothing," he said, in a tone that meant it was far from nothing.

She took his hand, slipping the warmth of her fingers into his. "I missed you," she said. "Far too much. You shouldn't have stayed away."

"Cass, I . . . even if all this wasn't happening, I wouldn't have enough years in my life to explain how sorry I am. The words just don't cover it."

"I know," she said, looking down at the grass in front of her feet. "It wasn't your fault."

He halted, in the shade of one of the trees. "What?" he said.

"It wasn't your fault, Wren," she said, raising her eyes up to meet his. "It was a mistake. Don't you think I worked that out? I know how it happened." She paused, and gave that faint, almost sorrowful smile again. "Still wanted to kill you, though."

"I'm—" he began, but she laid a finger on his lips.

"Don't," she said. "Enough apologies. I forgive you."

Wren's face broke into a smile of such childlike relief that Cass felt tears springing to her own eyes to match his. "You mean that?" he whispered.

"I mean it," she said. "But you shouldn't have stayed away so long, Wren. I didn't know how much you . . . meant to me. Until I saw you again, until you came round to my house. It shouldn't have gone this way, Wren. We should have stayed together, whatever."

And he knew then why she, like him, had made no effort to go back to her family during what could well be their last moments. It was communicated in her eyes, in the undertones of her words. And at that moment, he felt a terrible pang of loss, for all the time he had wasted hiding from her, unwilling to face this girl when he had known, all along, that she was the only one he had ever wanted. He had thought he had something with Kayleigh, but . . . maybe it had been only a distraction. Maybe he had been kidding himself. Maybe there *was* no other.

"I always loved you," he said, the words coming out more smoothly than he could have imagined possible. "That's why I couldn't face you being hurt."

"And that's why we're here now," she said. "This is fate working."

"You think so?"

"I know so."

For a moment, her eyes flickered away from his, and he saw in the dark pools of her pupils the bright cluster of stars tracking across the sky behind him. Missiles. She looked back at him, and her voice was brittle now.

"I'm scared, Wren," she said.

"So am I," he replied.

"Hold me."

He did. They closed their eyes and embraced, and the embrace turned to a kiss, long and slow and deep, a kiss loaded with all the longing for the lost hours they had thrown away. In amid the fear, there was a contentment and a *rightness* such as neither of them had ever felt before. Beyond that, all else was meaningless.

And behind them, a blinding flash cut across the horizon, lighting the inside of their eyelids with its fury.

Acknowledgements

ENDGAME was written with the help of the following books. Any scientific errors, mistakes, inconsistencies or foul-ups are purely due to the author's inability to read properly.

Larry Ephron; *The End*

Jon Erickson; *Ice Ages Past and Future*

Peter Griffiths; *Nuclear Weapons: The Last Great Debate*

Bernard Harbor and Chris Smith; *Points of View: Nuclear Weapons*

Bruce D Clayton; *Life After Doomsday: A Survivalist Guide to Nuclear War and Other Major Disasters*

Ivan Tyrell; *The Survival Option – A Guide to Living Through Nuclear War*

Patrick O'Heffeman; *The First Nuclear World War*

About the Author

Chris Wooding was born in Leicester in 1977 and his first book was published when he was just nineteen years old. He studied English Literature at Sheffield University and now lives in London. He has written several books, including the *Broken Sky* series, *Crashing*, *Kerosene*, *Catchman* and most recently the acclaimed novels *The Haunting of Alaizabel Cray* and *Poison*.

POISON

IT WAS Snapdragon's scream that jerked Poison awake. She half-rose out of her blankets, sloughing off a thin dusting of sparkling flakes that covered her. Strangely, despite the circumstances of her waking, she immediately felt the warm hand of sleep enfolding her again, making her eyes droop. She shook herself in puzzlement, looking down at the stuff on her blanket and in her hair. It was like unmelted snow, yet it glimmered in the cloudy light of the morning sun that came in through the round window.

She felt herself drowsing again, against her will, and this time she flung her blankets aside and pulled herself out of the tattered old bed. The flakes . . . it was something to do with the flakes. . . She did not understand how or why, but some instinct had made the connection between the mysterious stuff that covered the bed and the weight of slumber that pressed down on her. She tousled and shook her hair and patted down her hemp nightrobe frantically, as if trying to beat out flames, and she felt her tiredness lift from her as the flakes fell free. She stared at them in alarmed wonder for a moment.

"What have you *done?*" Snapdragon shrieked at her from

the other side of the small room, and Poison suddenly remembered why it was she had been awoken. Snapdragon was standing at Azalea's cradle, her face a rictus of horror, her eyes needling accusation at Poison.

Poison rubbed a hand across her face to smear the last remnants of sleep from her eyes and came over to the crib, ignoring Snapdragon completely. There was a terrible sinking in her chest, a spreading void of premonition.

She looked into the crib. Whatever it was that lay in there, it was not Azalea.

"Why didn't you wake?" Snapdragon hissed. "You were right there! You terrible thing! Why didn't you wake?"

Poison was not listening. The world seemed to have shrunk to the size of the crib, and what was inside it. Sounds had become faint, even Snapdragon's shrill voice in her ear. She could hear the slow whoosh of blood as it swept round her body, the inrush and release of her breath. She put her hands on the side of the crib to steady herself. Somewhere in her memory, a small silver bell was chiming.

She pushed herself away from the crib and snatched down the thickest tome on her bookshelf. She had borrowed it from Fleet a long time ago, and never thought to give it back. Its dusty leather cover creaked as she opened it, and the pages flickered under her fingers.

"Reading? Reading at a time like this?" Snapdragon howled. Poison spared her an annoyed glance before resuming her search. Her stepmother began to weep. "Poor Hew. What'll I tell him? What'll I say? His heart will break."

The page that Poison was looking for flipped flat, and she felt her head go light. There it was. The leftmost page was dominated by a black-and-white woodcut print of a hunched figure dressed in a long, ragged coat, its face shadowed under a wide-brimmed hat. Its eyes were two slits in the darkness. It held out before it one long, thin arm, and its scrawny, emaciated hand held a tiny bell delicately between thumb and forefinger. With its other hand, it was scattering something that looked like dust. In the picture, it was in a wooded glade, surrounded by sleeping people.

"The Scarecrow," she whispered.

Poison heard the chime again in her head. She frowned, puzzled, and stared hard at the page. Had she seen something *move* there, just a moment ago? She peered closer.

The picture suddenly seemed to grow under her gaze, as if she was falling into it or it was rising from the page to swallow her. The black-and-white leaves of the trees seemed to stir. She felt dizzy, her violet eyes going wide.

The Scarecrow turned its head to look at her, staring out from the page, and her throat tightened in terror. She wanted to close the book suddenly, but she could not will her muscles to move. She felt herself pinned there, unable to even blink. Disbelief and panic clawed their way upward from her chest.

The Scarecrow began to walk towards her. Its movements were curiously jerky, as if she was watching a flicker-book, but it was definitely moving. Coming closer in short, hobbling steps, its tiny bell held out before it.

Impossible, she told herself. *Impossible*.

But she could not draw back, could not look away. The chime sounded again as the Scarecrow twitched the bell, a pure and unutterably sinister note, quiet and yet clearer than anything else she could hear. It had loomed until its upper body almost filled the page now, as if she was looking at it through a window and it was almost at the sill. The bell chimed again, dominating her consciousness. The white slits of the Scarecrow's eyes burned into her from within the inky darkness of its face.

Poison could barely breathe. What air she could force into her lungs came in shudders. Everything she knew was telling her that this could not be happening, that it was only a picture on a page she was looking at; and yet the Scarecrow grew, shuffling closer and closer until it seemed that there was only the thickness of the page separating them.

It put one hand on the edge of the picture, and its fingers folded over the bottom of the page and scraped against her wrist.

The slam of the outside door jolted her out of her trance, and she flung the book away with a cry. It tumbled to the floor and landed shut with a heavy thump on the planks. Trembling, she stared at it from her bed, ready to run if it should do anything other than lie where it was.

Nothing happened.

Poison felt her heartbeat decelerate slowly, and began to breathe again. She clasped her hands in her lap to try and stop them shaking, stealing glances at the book now and again. There must be an explanation, there must be. . .

It was then that she noticed that Snapdragon was gone, and married that realization to the slam of the hut door she had heard a moment ago. The crib was empty too.

In a flash, she saw what Snapdragon was going to do; and she scrambled off her bed and fled out of the door to try and stop her.

∾∾

It was a cold and dank morning, the sun clambering up through the faintly greenish miasma that hung over the Black Marshes. A little early still for the flies to be out, for the waters of the marsh had not yet warmed to the day's heat. Poison emerged from her hut into the chill, clad only in her hemp nightdress. It did not bother her overly: most of the village was still abed after the excitement of Soulswatch Eve, and though she looked faintly ridiculous, her nightdress was thicker and warmer than her daywear and she did not care what the villagers thought anyway. She had the sense to pause to put on some boots though, for it was virtually suicide to walk barefoot in the mud of the marsh, where there were insects and snakes, venomous spiders and spiny snails underfoot, any of which could kill with a bite or a scratch.

Snapdragon was nowhere to be seen, but there was only one bridge from their platform to the next, so she hurried over it to her neighbour's platform, where the wraith-catcher snored in Bluff's house while Bluff and his wife made do with the floor. Two rope bridges branched off from there; one of them was still swinging slightly in the wake of Snapdragon's passage. Poison took it, already knowing where Snapdragon was going.

She caught sight of her stepmother just as she was disappearing into the trees that crowded up against the lake in which Gull stood. The thing that had been in the crib was wrapped up tight in a blanket, held against her chest. Poison called out to her as she ran on to the rope-bridge that spanned the murky water from shore to village. Snapdragon paused momentarily and looked back, and there was a kind of madness in her expression; then she plunged on into the trees. Poison rushed after her and slipped on the moist planking of the bridge, but she caught the ropes at either side with her armpits before she could fall, and she suffered only sore burns on her skin. Cursing herself, she ran on and into the marsh.

The ground squelched beneath her boots as she followed Snapdragon. This was relatively solid ground as far as the Black Marshes went, and she knew it to be mercifully free of bogs and sinkholes. She caught a glimpse of her stepmother's blonde braid swinging ahead of her through the trees. Something crunched under her boot, but she did not stop to see what unfortunate creature she had stepped on. The trees had been chopped back a little way here, forming a bumpy trail that had been flattened down by innumerable feet. She put on speed and began catching up with Snapdragon, who was slowing as she ran out of breath, until by the time they got to the well Poison was almost close enough to touch her.

The well sat in the middle of a roughly hewn clearing, a stone-lined shaft with square walls that rose out of the ground to waist-height. A tight, rusty grille lay over the shaft, and a roof above that. The roof was sloped inward to a funnel, so that any rainwater it caught was spouted down into the shaft. Rainwater was fine, and so was the clear water from the underground spring that the well fed off; but they did not want any of the murky surface pollution of the marsh to get into their precious drinking supply, nor any slimy marsh creatures to fall in, hence the wall and the grille.

Snapdragon stumbled to her knees as she entered the clearing, dropping her burden to the soft earth. It made not a sound. When Poison reached her, she was hyperventilating great whoops of air.

"Here, here, do this," Poison said, her impatient tone masking real concern. She pulled Snapdragon's sleeve over her hand and put it to her stepmother's mouth. "Hold that."

Snapdragon did so with her free hand while Poison pulled the sleeve tight at her elbow, cutting off the air and making a reasonable cloth bag for Snapdragon to breathe into. She gasped a little more, but soon she was breathing normally again, and finally Poison let her go.

"You shouldn't get so excited," Poison advised.

Snapdragon sagged, her eyes falling to the bundle on the ground before her. "It's so heavy," she said.

Poison looked at where it lay, eerily still. She had wrapped it up like a loaf of bread. She wondered whether it was breathing or not. Then she wondered if it needed to.

"You were going to put it in the well?" she asked.

"I can't let Hew see it! It would kill him!"

"Don't be an idiot!" Poison snapped back. "For one thing, you'd pollute the water supply if you left it rotting down there; hadn't you thought of that? Besides, you can't drown it. Don't you know what that thing is?"

Snapdragon gave her a furious glare. She hated being made to feel ignorant. "I suppose *you* do?"

"It's a changeling," Poison said. "A changeling. And if you'd put it down that well, we'd never get Azalea back."

Snapdragon looked at her in disbelief. "How do you know? How do you *know*, you little witch? Did you do it to her? Did you?"

Poison did not bother to answer that. Instead, she scooped up the bundle – and it *was* heavy, like carrying stone rather than flesh – and looked down on where Snapdragon had begun to sob in the mud, her dress slimed and ruined.

"Say nothing of this. I will deal with it."

"Where has Azalea gone? What are you going to do?" Snapdragon called after her as she walked away.

"Say nothing of this," Poison called back, partly because she wanted Snapdragon to understand how important that was, partly because she did not know the answer to either of her questions.

But one man would.

CRASHING

Chris Wooding

So here it was – the party to mark the beginning of the summer. I guess we'd all brought our own agendas; mine was to get it together with Jo Anderson.

But everyone knows stuff like that never goes to plan. Friends were rapidly turning into enemies. The local mob of street-thug wannabes had declared virtual war on me. And looming over it all was the spectre of the Zone, the derelict estate haunted by stoners, psychos and freaks, calling me back one last time. Now I just needed to get my friends on board...

KEROSENE

Chris Wooding

Cal's got this thing about fire. It's nothing
big at first, just lighting matches, watching them
burn, enjoying the calming effects of the flame...
It helps him cope with stuff.

Then he meets Abby, and things start
to get out of control. She winds him up, playing
with him until he thinks he might lose his sanity, and
suddenly the matches just aren't enough any more.
So a plan hatches itself in Cal's mind, a plan so
glorious it could set the world alight.
Nothing will ever touch him again...

THE
HAUNTING
OF
ALAIZABEL CRAY

Chris Wooding

**Amongst the dark streets of London
dwells unimaginable terror…**

It happened after the Vernichtung – the war
left the city damaged, bruised, battered, its people
shattered and battle-scarred, and open
to a terrifying retribution…

Foul things lurk within the labyrinth of the Old
Quarter, and those who venture out at night are easy
prey. Prey for the wolves and murderers that stalk
the crooked streets, and for creatures far
more deadly – the wych-kin.

But evil disguised is deadliest of all.
And behind the façade of wealth and charity that
surrounds the uppermost levels of society lies
a terrifying pact with the wych-kin that
threatens humankind's very existence.

At its heart is the beautiful, vulnerable,
enigmatic Alaizabel Cray – key to the ultimate evil.